Other books by Advance Concept Design Books for Bryant Val Jeane Faubion:

The Second Daisy Queen
Texas Short Stories

The Diary of the Beans

by

Bryant Val Jeane Faubion

Advanced Concept Design Books
Lago Vista, TX

This is a work of historical semi-fiction. Historical individuals and places and events are mentioned. Villages are actual name places. All other characters, locales, and accounts of events are fictional and are entirely the product of the imagination of the author, and any similarities are purely coincidental.

CID, Inc.
6706 Bar K Ranch Rd.
Lago Vista, TX 78645

Published by arrangement with
Advanced Concept Design Books, an imprint of
CID, Inc. Tx

Library of Congress Control Number
to be assigned
International Standard Book Number
ISBN 13: 978-0-9799723-2-4
ISBN 10: 0-9799723-2-9

For information, address
bvjfaubion@advancedconceptdesign.com
First paperback printing November 2007
Printed in the United States of America

Forward

This book is about spirits and events from 1890 to 1965 in the Big Bend area of the Rio Grande as it flows between Mexico and West Texas. The land is mesas of ancient limestones and shales and much younger mountains and spires of igneous rock which rose from inside the earth three hundred billion hours ago. (Dinosaurs became extinct about five hundred and seventy billion hours ago). That volcanic activity also formed dikes and underground structures in the fractured and faulted sedimentary rock. Springs can be found in the driest parts of this desert landscape, and the intricate subterranean geology still hides the routes and sources of these waters. Hidden caverns and grottoes provide shade and water to only those who have wandered the land to discover its many secrets. This story is about the only man who knew them all—Juan Pablo Luna. And, it is the story of the only woman he ever loved, the courageous and daring Consuelo Alvarez.

CHAPTER 1

For the first time in his life, 27 year old entomologist Gene Hart felt the sun as a deadly, enormous, raging nuclear furnace. The once benevolent giver of the golden tan now seemed intent upon broiling him.

Setting out early that morning, he had hiked into a rugged and isolated area of the Big Bend known as the Solitario, while the last of his water had slowly dripped from his second canteen, the hot drops falling onto his backpack to vaporize into the hot, dry air as he had climbed over and between the Solitario's upthrust rock formations. He was searching for as yet undiscovered varieties of water beetles to be found in the temporary streams and natural catch basins found in this part of the Great Chihuahua Desert, where spring rain had brought him to believe that all the water beetle community should be thriving and experiencing a population explosion.

Absorbed in the hunt, his mouth was already dry when he reached for the second of his two canteens and found it drained. He felt an urge to keep seeking a water beetle habitat. Water would be there and he could drink, but he knew he must immediately give up the search and start back for his pickup where there was a cooler of water and beer.

He was already beginning to dehydrate as the noon sun brought the air temperature to over a hundred breezeless degrees. The rock surfaces were much hotter, and he felt their heat radiating onto his exposed skin. He reached for the compass in his shirt pocket.

He lifted the compass out and opened its lid to discover that the needle had come off its mount. He tried to shake it upside down, then bounced the compass in his hand, trying to get the needle back in place. Then, using his fingers, he tried to pry off the glass cover so he could set the needle in place, but the cover suddenly pulled free and the needle flew through the air to land unseen on the gravel strewn ground. After an unsuccessful search , he decided he knew which way was west, and he hurriedly set out. Then, as he approached the top of a mound of loose stone and gravel, he fell and slid back to the bottom, spraining an ankle.

"I'm going to die out here," he joked to himself in a flat voice without any real feeling that death was possible. "No, I can make it back to the truck if I don't waste anymore time."

Just after he said those words, a nauseating rush of deja vu insisted that he had been through this before. "Damn," he said, "I've been through this before? Apparently I live through this. If I had not lived through it, I wouldn't have known it was deja vu. Got to get moving. Maybe this ankle will make me more careful. The sprain is a good thing," he assured himself as he again made his way up the slope. But the trip took three times as long as before.

It was late afternoon when he fully realized he was not thinking clearly. For the last hour he had limped along without thoughts of anything but the water jug in the truck, and he had lost awareness of direction. "I am going to die," he said loudly. He was greatly affected by the thought. Immediately, almost while saying those words, he felt a sense of starkness, and he began to shiver as the primitive area of his brain precipitated a dose of adrenalin. “This is deja vu,” he yelled out. “You can't die in a deja vu. How could you,” he asked himself in an assuring voice?

Rationality sobered him for a moment, then he began to believe that he felt the bombarding solar radiation as a weight combining with gravity, squeezing the third dimension from him. He foresaw his body as flat as a fried egg laying on the baked ground with his belly exposed like a pink yolk which grew flatter and redder as it cooked.

Fantasizing a hidden jug of water, he took off his pack only to find among its contents some specimen bottles, a notebook, a camera. He frantically emptied the pack onto the ground. There, he noticed liquid in two of the specimen bottles. “The distilled water,” he said loudly. “I've got distilled water. Belly up to the bar, boys,” he shouted in a raspy voice. He downed the three ounces of hot water in one of the bottles and it seemed to absorb into his tongue and not even wet his throat. “That won't do it,” he said. He looked at the second bottle and decided to save it for later.

The mouth of water brought him a

moment of lucidity. He knew the sun would kill him if he could not find a cool, shaded spot and hole-up until it set. “It's almost a full moon tonight, he said confidently. “I'd be able to read an Archie comic book.” He visualized Veronica in a red, white polka dot bikini. “The moon will rise in the east and I'll simply walk west to Fresno Creek and downstream to the truck. Maybe I can collect some dew when it cools off.”

Thoughts of fine art began to parade through his increasingly irrational mind as he limped along. He quickly wheeled through his favorites, from cave drawings to Cubism. Then he began to speak, so the artists could hear—the ones he believed to be hiding among the rocks. Under his breath he said, “One never can tell when they were around or not. No. I'm sure some are here and hiding in the shade. All I have to do is find a shady spot, throw the artist in it out, and wait for sundown. I don’t think there is any artist here big enough to take me. Any shade will be all mine. But, still, thank heavens I'm xeric, for, if I were not, I'd be dead and rising as torn pieces in feathered bellies lifted by the next thermal.”

For a moment he admired his poetic words, then he wondered if xeric was the right word to use, then a tight smile stretched his stuck-together lips as he stood swaying in the sun.

"But." He spun completely around on one foot while he exclaimed the word. "What art do I like right now?" A rocking chair subliminally appeared in his vision as he began to sing, "Go down Moses, way down to Egypt land; tell O' Pharoah to let my people go."

"I like Whistler's Grandmother," he declared loudly. "Actually, I think I like his mother most. Yeah. I don't admire his grandmother. I like his mother. There's something in her rocker I need to see to survive. There's a shaded artist in a rocker around here someplace. Is that my pack on the ground? My pack has turned into a rock. No. That's my camera by the pack rock. I've found my way back to my stuff. And I thought I was lost. Hah!"

He slung his camera strap over his shoulder and wandered off, staggering toward the bottom of one of the Solitario's concentric rings of ridges. He looked around for cover and noticed a jumble of huge rocks above him which appeared to hold places shaded and full of coolth. He felt the shirt pocket which held the last bottle of water and patted his camera. "I want to die with my camera on," he said loudly, and he began to climb upward. As he crawled onto a boulder he noticed that he had ceased to sweat and suddenly felt very dizzy. "Heat stroke," he babbled to himself. Seeing a place under an overhanging rock which was large enough to crawl under, he scooted down the side of a boulder, and, with blurring vision, he found a shady entrance. Crawling on his hands and knees, he discovered that the overlaying boulders hid an even deeper recess that turned to the left, became tunnel-like, and led into a darkness with a cool draft coming out of it. Between him and the darkness, the floor beyond the entrance was missing, and he could crawl no farther. He settled his back against the cool wall and closed his eyes to rest.

He felt better out of the heat, and a twinge of rationality returned. He began to think about dying so far away from his home and friends, and thought maybe he should return to his backpack so somebody could at least find his remains. He visualized his girlfriend. She was standing over a skeleton wearing a camera and saying, "Yes, that's Gene's camera, alright."

His mind continued to wander, "How far am I from home? Let me see. I'm a long way. A long way from that place in space where Earth was on the day I was born—a long way from June 1937 to April 1965. That place in space is my real home. I'll bet it's cool there right now; far away from any sun, in the comfort of no gravity. Just cool starlight and me there. My space womb, cool and pleasant with waterlight and sweet waterberries —the kind the Milky Way grows best. I've got a waterberry," he mumbled with the tone of revelation, and he downed the last specimen bottle of water.

The sun left the Solitario with Gene babbling alone in its arid vastness. A waxing moon appeared and floated upward as he tried to stay awake, but he did not think about leaving, or even moving. He was happy where he was, with sweet waterberries all around him, there in his original astral home. A shaft of moon appeared in the darkness farther into the tunnel, but he could not see it.

Half asleep, he began to hallucinate torrents of rain and walls of water rushing down a dry arroyo. Then, dreaming, he struggled rapidly up the arroyo's side and stumbled into a cave just as clear blue water flooded by. He pulled off his soaked shirt and, holding it above his head, wrung out mouthfuls of fresh water. He wrung the shirt tightly for every drop, saving none, for he knew there was plenty more in his pants. Then, he saw photons as large as grapes shooting down from the sun. They bounced and ricocheted about, and they rained down into the blue water-filled arroyo causing the water to dance and hiss and steam until it was again dust dry.

He heard a voice, "You need water. Look, your pants have dried out before you could drink them."

Gene, conscious again, still sitting against the rock where he first rested, turned his head toward a vision whose soothing, female voice came from farther inside the cave. Then, he saw a translucent figure of a woman emerge from the darkness. She wore a typical goddess gown revealing her outline of feminine curves. His left eye, which was not swollen shut with salt and sand, completed tracing her outline and coloring-in the missing parts when he asked, "Who are you?"

He heard her reply, "I am the wood nymph, Dytiscidae."

He began a conversation, "But, there are no woods here. This is no place for a wood nymph."

"It was when I was exiled to this place after my side lost a little theomachy. It was a forest, then. A little on the dry side, but there was running water. Look inside this cave and you will find branches of trees brought here by forest creatures. This was once a place of great trees, and I presided over its cool green shade. I am not of hours, and centuries are like days to me. One day I awoke in this cave and it was all desert outside."

He replied, "There are forests close to here, in the Chisos Mountains. Can't you go there?"

Melodramatically placing her forearm over her brow, and speaking with the pained voice of a reminiscing exile from paradise, "I cannot get there. By day I must travel bower to bower in the shade under a canopy of leaves, for my body sublimates in the Egyptian god's direct light, and my spirit evaporates in a treeless night to be diluted, becoming lifeless mist among the myriad of stars."

He asked, "How long have you been in here?"

"For you, thousands of years; for me, merely days, and in another few days I will awake in a forest of oaks and madronnes, then, by afternoon, I will be in a deep forest of great pines and firs rising above green ferns. Go to sleep and awake with me among the trees on shaded banks beside flowing clear water." Then, he heard her thoughts as she had an aside in her mind, "Hell, I think I'll actually do just that."

The vision turned and began to float into the cave. He said, "No. Don't go," and began to get up. His head bashed into the rock ceiling and he fell back to his sitting position. He felt a trickle of blood on his forehead and wiped his finger through it. He tasted it. "I could drink my blood," he thought. "It's just red water like the liquid from ripe waterberries on the infrared end of the vine."

His last vision was of the snake which was looped and devouring itself. With each breath, his blood became a bit thicker, and gradually thoughts and delusions faded away and he was unconscious and undreaming.

CHAPTER 2

"Vagabundo, wake up. The sun will be finding us soon." The Cactus Man stood up above his bedroll and stretched his arms up, then he bent forward and backward to stretch his back muscles. He knew his burro liked the day to begin with the same words; that it reassured the animal that all was normal and the day would be a usual day. Vagabundo, who liked to hear his name, stood close by in the cold, dark, early morning, with his long ears directed at his companion, waiting to hear what the burro knew should be the next words as the man lit a breakfast fire fueled by dried, cow manure and withered grass. The Cactus Man then uttered the expected words in the expected tone, "My, you are a fine looking burro this morning. I am lucky to have such a good companion."

The sun would be up in another forty-five minutes, but it would still be behind the closest hill to their east. Several coyotes had scurried farther away upon hearing his voice, and cactus wrens began to call as the cloudless sky began to lighten. “All the spirits must be asleep here, or maybe none live here, since I had no dreams last night. Did you, Vagabundo?”

Today, the man would continue gathering small ornamental cactus plants in the Bofecillos Mountains about twenty rugged miles of back country west northwest of Terlingua, Texas. The area they traveled had received spring rain and the flowering tips of the tall, thin stalks of ocotillo were like scarlet flames. Prickly pear cactuses were full of delicate, silky, brightly colored blossoms which seemed to be their apologies for sharp thorns covering their pads, and for the clusters of tiny spines which grew on the fruit and swelled the tongues of hungry cattle.

A family of Spanish Daggers, standing like solid shadows looming against a predawn, indigo sky, seemed to be watching the man tie his bedroll above the canvas bags strapped to Vagabundo's sides. The man could sense times when the desert's plants were aware of him, and he began to speak to them as he poured oats for Vagabundo into a tin pie plate,

"We know what you plants are saying, don't we Vagabundo?"

The burro only heard the air and the birds and the man, but the man heard the plants answer, "Someday you will be one of us again. Someday you will be earth again, and our seeds will grow you into one of us, and you will no longer fear the sun."

"Someday is not today, is it Vagabundo?" He drank a mouthful of hot, weak coffee from a metal, canteen cup, went to the closest Spanish Dagger, scooped out a shallow depression at its base, and poured a drink of coffee into it. As it sucked into the sand, he stood up and told the plant, which was his height, "See what you are missing. Next time I am this way, and you are full of flowers, I will give your children some coffee with sugar. Children love sugar. And someday when I am a plant and you are a people, remember, I like my coffee without sugar."

He had an appointment in Lajitas, Texas in four days for the once a month meeting with the woman who had bought cactus from him for the past ten years. On this trip he would enter the Solitario where he would visit places only he knew. One of them was a place with the rarest of all the plants he had ever discovered; the ones he called the Segundon. But he would not linger at the hard to reach site, for the Solitario also held one of the secret places where he cached the cosas antiguas (old things) he had come upon during his sixty years crisscrossing alkaline flats and exploring every valley, ravine, and mountain side of the Big Bend.

His life had been spent where the sun gave life sparingly, and generously brought death to any creature unprepared or weakened. His body had toughened through exposure to be resistant to the sun's unrelenting thirst for anything liquid. His skin was thick, impermeable, and, in his old age, always shaded by layers of cotton khaki clothing and a wide-brimmed khaki hat.

To him the desert was full of spirits, but they were those of the living and once living plants, animals, and people. He knew the sun was not a spirit. It was not evil or benevolent and would desiccate the devilish and the angelic, the coyote and the rabbit, without regard. He knew the sun and moon and earth as unthinking, unfeeling, and blameless for what they were and for their effects upon the living, but he would still talk to them. Knowing something was spiritless and mindless did not stop this avid conversationalist from addressing it.

Of the succession of five burros he had traveled with through the years, Vagabundo was the only one who would always listen to the Cactus Man's every word, and this was very important because a burro had been his only companion since the life he once shared long ago with his twin brother, and since a time seeming even longer ago, with his only love, Consuelo Alvarez.

The Cactus Man talked much of the time, and often reminded the burro that everyone likes a good listener. He told Vagabundo about the plants they passed, and, when they were where something once happened which was tragic or poignant or otherwise memorable, he would retell the story to the attentive burro who would listen, directing his ears at the words, with his eyes seeming to stare back into the time of the event; eyes which told the Cactus Man that his friend had a feeling for the face of time that even he could not always have, anymore. That caused him to wonder who the plants had been which had made the milk Vagabundo suckled from his mother.

Direct sunshine struck them as they walked toward Fresno Canyon. In the high desert there is a quick transition from the cold of night to the heat of day. When the sunshine is direct, its heat almost instantly replaces the cold of the dawn. He sat down on a rock and removed his hat, momentarily, and held it to shade his eyes from the sun. “You have found us again,” he said. The light on his face displayed to any new local spirits its burnt color, like that land's igneous rock which intruded the dinosaur's graveyard of limestone and shale. The old man’s oiled bronze face showed scars and deep lines seeming to map the paths of a lifetime spent walking that rugged landscape. Sitting motionless by the grazing burro, he appeared to be stone and earth fused with one of the area's gnarled, rough-barked, canyon oaks, which in winter seemed dead and dry, but were alive inside with life's juices.

A person could be close to him and not be aware of a presence, and indeed many, including Big Bend park rangers, had unknowingly passed within easy sight of him as he stood, infused with the spirit of a plant, or sat, weighted with the solidness of stone.

Still sitting, he put on a pair of Lolita-style sunglasses with red, heart shaped frames— one of a carton of fifty pair he had traded a box of cactuses for while in Study Butte in 1964. He had wanted them because the lenses were extra dark, and it came to be that Vagabundo liked them. And the Cactus Man enjoyed watching people's faces when he appeared in Study Butte wearing them. He also enjoyed the company of the butterflies and humming birds attracted by the bright red rims. He stood up and stretched his back muscles again, then the dusty khaki clothes with the bronze man inside, wearing the incredible sunglasses, began walking east through a land of sun and stone.

They were about three miles south-southeast of Saucito Spring, heading for a cattle trail leading to the bottom of Fresno Canyon, which lay between them and the

Solitario. They moved slowly as Vagabundo halted to graze patches of grass freshly greened from a localized shower. After an hour of narrating, grazing, and walking, they began to work their way down the switchback trail to the canyon bottom where, even if the creek was not running, they knew where water was to be found.

Fresno creek was not bone-dry, but there was no flowing water. Vagabundo drank from a puddle while Cactus Man walked to a seeping spring at the base of a cliff a short distance up a side-canyon. The water emerged only to flow a few feet and submerge again. He caught the dribbling water in Vagabundo's oat pan, poured it into his empty canteen, and checked to be sure his other five were full. He felt the little burro nuzzle his hat as the man drank down a pan of spring water.

After drinking and eating a snack of leftover pancakes, they headed up the east side of the canyon on a cattle trail leading to the first of the arroyo-breached rings of rock which encircled the Solitario. There were easier ways to enter, but he was going to a specific spot, and he knew the easiest route to it was not along one of the two canyons which led to the center. They worked their way along a cattle trail, then up a rocky slope, through a gap, and down into an area between two of the many weathered, arcing ridges of limestone.

It was almost noon and the Cactus Man was moving through the rocks as rapidly as he could. He wanted to be where the cosas antiguas were located when the sun was directly above, for it was then that the sunlight, streaming through a narrow, long slit in the rock ceiling, lit the floor of the place the cosas were stored.

Just before twelve they arrived at the spot where Vagabundo knew to wait while the Cactus Man climbed up a ledge and over car-sized rocks, then descended to the hiding place's entrance. Vagabundo watched as the man disappeared from view, then he heard his friend loudly exclaim, “Madre de Dios,” and appear again and scramble down the hillside.

He told the burro, “The sun has sucked someone almost dry, but he still lives.” He lifted a canteen from the packsaddle and grabbed the tin cup and a cafe-sized packet of sugar, and one of salt, and again climbed to the entrance.

Gene Hart's first vision was of a butterfly with wings like two red hearts hovering just beside him. He would have been startled but he was too weak to start, and he simply mumbled, “What the hell.”

The Cactus Man kept pouring sips of water into Hart's mouth, and after fifteen minutes the man began to animate. He placed his hands around the cup and drank it dry.

The Cactus Man refilled the cup. While the man drank, Cactus Man removed his sunglasses and looked into the passage and saw a cobweb still stretched across from side to side. He knew the man had not gone any farther than the drop-off where a four foot wide breach separated the entrance from the chamber beyond.

“I am called the Cactus Man,” he told him. “The sun almost sucked you dry.”

“How did you find me? Is there someone out looking for me?”

“Was there anybody with you. Is the sun killing somebody else out there?”

“No. Like a fool I hiked in alone,

looking for bugs that live in water. Pretty funny, huh."

"Some funny things happen in this desert, and some not so funny things. I suppose you parked your ride on the road to Presidio? I will guide you back there when you feel strong enough. Where are your sunglasses?"

Hart replied, "I think I dropped them somewhere while I wandered around in circles."

"I have some extras on my burro; I will give you one. You need sunglasses in these bright rocks. You need to shade your eyes. A professor from somewhere told me that."

On the way out, they came upon the backpack and its poured out contents. The Cactus Man re-packed the gear, placed the pack on Vagabundo, and they continued along cattle trails to the parked truck where they arrived four hours later.

On the way the Cactus Man had insisted that Gene wear a wet cloth draped over his head and shoulders. By the time they arrived at the truck he had poured three canteens of water over the cloth and had reminded Gene a dozen times that he had to keep his brain cool after the sun had dried it out.

Another truck was parked close by, and the two people inside stared at the men emerging from the canyon—one limping, one pouring water on the limping man's head, and both wearing Lolita sunglasses.

At his truck Gene offered the Cactus Man money for helping him, but he refused it.

Then, the Cactus Man said, “I know what you can do, if you like. Loan me your camera and a closeup lens and I will take some pictures for you of some water bugs like you have maybe never seen before. I call them, pecas, and I have only found them in one place.”

Hart thought this was the Cactus Man's way of asking for his camera as a reward. “Sure he said, I'll load it with fresh film and put on a closeup lens. Maybe you'll need the regular lens, too. Here,” he gratefully handed the camera and lenses to him. “By the way, how do you know about closeup lenses? Are you a photographer?”

The Cactus Man said, “National

Geographic has been all over this place. I showed them things and they showed me things. I will be in Lajitas at the store on Saturday before noon, and I will have your stuff and pictures. Do not forget you are wearing those silly sunglasses when you get to town."

Gene thought about the entire episode as he watched the man and burro walk away. He said to himself, "I'll bet he's not at Lajitas Saturday. I'll be there just to see. Possibly he's trustworthy. Oh, for God's sake, man, he saved your life. Let him have the camera."

CHAPTER 3

The Cactus Man and Vagabundo spent the night in Fresno Canyon, and the next morning were again heading for the site of the cosas antiguas. They arrived and Vagabundo watched as his companion climbed upward and disappeared within the jumble of boulders. The burro directed his ears and waited for the unusual to happen again, but all sounded normal and he began to relax.

Cactus Man crawled into the entrance past the place where he had found Gene. He reached up onto a ledge and pulled down an eight foot plank, with which, he bridged the crevasse. He crawled across and continued to crawl until he could stand up.

The sun was just beginning to touch the floor, but the line of light was only as wide as a pencil. He unrolled a length of white cloth and positioned it where the band of light would be broadest in its transit, and waited for the sun to arrive upon the cloth and fill the chamber with soft light.

As the sunlight moved onto the cloth, and the beam broadened, the features of the grotto appeared. It was a room about the size and height of a small adobe dwelling. Water emerging from the base of a wall dribbled ripples into a clear pool about ten feet in diameter. At the pool's other end the water flowed over a dike of black stone and streamed into a fissure. Part of the line of light had entered the water, and water bugs, the pecas, swarmed into it to sun themselves.

He readied the camera and photographed the orange speckled bugs as they swam in the light. He, also, took some pictures of the yellow and green striped minnows who swam with the pecas. Using up the roll of film, he put away the camera and went to the corner where he had arranged the cosas antiguas.

When the Cactus Man found it in 1953, it seemed that the grotto had been unvisited for many years. But, somebody long ago had already placed things there. Wrapped in the remnants of a moldered leather bag, he had found Spanish silver coins and jewelry with precious stones. The grotto also held a fifteen inch tall silver crucifix with a solid gold Jesus. The letters, MDCCXXV, were inscribed on its base, and it set on a ledge beyond the pool where someone unknown had placed it.

The Cactus Man took a mirror from his pocket and reflected the sunlight onto the crucifix, and again was overcome by the sight of the sparkling gold figure and the clusters of glistening precious stones on the ends of the cross and in the crown of thorns.

He stared at the object for a while, then placed Gene's leaky canteen and a chrome, truck horn onto a pile of junk he had collected and carried to the grotto. "Maybe I'm a pack rat," he surmised. He knew the grotto spirits did not like long visits and that it was time to leave before he became unwelcome, besides, he was thirsty, and he knew not to drink the peca's bad tasting water. He rolled up the strip of white cloth and grabbed the camera and departed.

He heard the lonely burro braying below as he worked his way under and over and around the rocks which had kept the grotto a secret. Upon his arrival, Vagabundo directed his ears toward him, which indicated to the

Cactus Man that the burro wanted to again hear the story about the grotto.

"I know, I know, you never get tired of the story about the cave of the silver crucifix? I have told it to you a hundred times. You know it better than me," he said as they walked eastward. The burro nudged him in the back, and the man answered, "Okay. Okay, I will tell it again. Before you were born, while you were still some plants, before I knew the finest burro in all creation would someday be my good friend and companion, I was with an ornery burro named Samson. It was 1953 and a cold December day when I saw a tiny cloud of vapor coming out of the rocks I climbed upon . . . ."

In two days he planned to arrive in the all but deserted village of Terlingua. Along his way he would visit the Solitario's unique cactus, the Segondon, but he would not sleep near them because of unsettling dreams carried by the spirits there.

The Segondon grew in a dark soil with emerald green specks throughout, and the area was cooler than the surrounding desert sand. The four inch tall cactuses each had five sides and was naked except for five stiff spines, one protruding straight up from the top of each of the five segments. In the center, below where the segments touched shoulders, lay pink lips holding a white sphere the size of a small pearl. Setting among the Segondon were five, goat-sized, igneous rocks which formed a twenty foot circle, and all of this had led the Cactus Man to believe that more than nature had been at work there.

In the past, when he had spent the night among the Segondon, the spirits had brought him dreams which he would not again endure. On the first night, Consuelo Alvarez, clothed in robes, moved among the five stones. She would lift and move each stone as if it were paper. Under the first she found the stock of a gun. Under the second she found the barrel of a gun. Under the third stone was a dove which flew and entered her chest, and, then, she grew angel wings. Consuelo the angel retrieved a single bullet from under the fourth stone. Then, as she lifted the final stone and set it to the side, a human figure rose from the hole the stone had covered. The figure said, "I am either Juan or Pablo, but not both. Then,

Consuelo assembled the gun, chambered the bullet and gave the loaded gun to the figure who then shot a shower of sparks, leaving Consuelo's wings in flames—burned and gone.

The Cactus Man, in anguish from the dream, but wanting to identify the figure, had slept among the Segondon the following night. The spirits placed him in a second dream, in which he could clearly feel there was something unknown which his brother had given him. His twin's face became a Bible, and upon opening it, he had found the pages to be mirrors on which, as he thumbed through them, each reflection would fade away before he could identify himself or another. The last page of mirrors showed a reflection which did not fade. It was of a person looking away from the page, and that faceless image said, "You see who killed an angel. Now have mercy and go find the child of the plant which will host the spirit of Consuelo Alvarez."

The Cactus Man had to fight his way from this second night's dream as he repeatedly traveled within it from beginning to end. Twisting and writhing in his bedroll, his hand had fallen upon the spikes of a Segondon, and he awoke with physical pain saving him from further anguish. In the morning he saw the Segondon which had saved him from being tortured all night. The cup which held its lips and pearl was full of blood.

CHAPTER 4

The Cactus Man had camped for the night on the eastern edge of the Solitario. Lajitas was just 14 miles due south of his camp, but it was only Thursday and he had until Saturday noon to arrive there to sell Vagabundo's load of cactuses and return Gene's camera.

An hour before sunrise Vagabundo heard the words he expected to hear. The Cactus Man built a fire and cooked breakfast. After pancakes, he poured a tired plant with children a drink of coffee, then the burro led the way as they headed out in a southeast direction, as usual, toward Sawmill Canyon to collect some of the fuzzy cactuses which grew there.

The sun found them as they were passing a hillock of dark igneous rock protruding above the shallow ravines cut through layers of the eroded limestone they walked through, and as usual, when first found, the Cactus Man sat down on a rock.

Vagabundo paused and looked back at him and was puzzled because his companion had not followed the ritual and removed his hat. The man sat in silence for such a long time that Vagabundo, tired of waiting for the expected words, continued toward the beds of cactuses. He was a hundred yards away when he returned to the man and nuzzled him, seeking what was wrong.

The Cactus Man looked up at the animal, and for a time did not know what the creature was, then did not know why a burro was standing by him. For a few minutes the man sat without knowing who he was, then his mind and memory all came back to him. He placed his Lolitas over his eyes and stood up and began to follow Vagabundo. The Cactus Man vaguely realized something had just happened, but he did not remember what it was, and the sun seemed to be higher in the sky than it should be.

On the southern side of the canyon at an interface of volcanic rock, and limestone which was many millions of years older, he surveyed a bed of the spherical, fist-sized cactuses to determine if he could harvest some without endangering the colony's future. He then dug up fifteen of a size he referred to as "teenagers." He placed them in Vagabundo's canvas bags while he told the cactuses how they would be planted in beautiful gardens and be pampered.

It was late afternoon when he decided to camp close by for part of the night and then walk to Terlingua in the early morning moonlight.

He slept with a dreamless mind, even though Sawmill Canyon was alive with spirits.

It was three in the morning when his breakfast fire appeared as a point of light to a family of rabbit hunters above the canyon. They had already smelled the delicious scent of burro, and, as salt pork sizzled in the skillet, the coyotes sniffed the mouth-watering air and wished they were wolves—a pack that could descend on the man's camp, scare him away, and devour the burro and the breakfast.

Vagabundo, not listening to the coyotes, awaited to hear the expected first words of the man. The burro was pleased when the routine proceeded normally. The early hour did not seem strange to Vagabundo, since, on treks across the Big Bend's lowland, lethally hot deserts, they would begin the journey well before the sun found them. And on the lands which were now called Big Bend National Park, they only traveled and worked by night because the park rangers did not seem to want them on the land they were born upon.

At six a.m. they arrived among the abandoned mine entrances on the back edge of Terlingua. They traveled through the flagstone and adobe ruins of houses whose occupants the man had known when the village was a living place of fifteen hundred people, and they paused at the ruins of the mercantile store. The Cactus Man sat down on a crumbled wall while the burro stared at him, waiting for some of the words which made his world secure and predictable. The man's thoughts, however, were not spoken as emotions came to him in memories of faces and love and pain and fiestas and struggles and encounters with vicissitudes which come with such intensity when people share a raw life together on the edge of the world.

The Cactus Man had shopped in the mercantile store when it was new. He had known Caprina and Guadalupe Hernandez when they began building the store in 1914, forty years before he came to be called the Cactus Man. He had witnessed the village as it began to grow with the mines, and he saw most families rush away when the quicksilver mining waned. He had lived there for a while after that, with a few hundred people who had no place to go, then he abandoned the village with others who could escape when the village quickly died with much suffering as the U.S. Immigration Service began raiding the Big Bend and deporting all they caught who could not prove they were born on the north side of the Rio Grande.

He would have the day to rest, then spend the night within the remnants of an adobe first occupied by him and his twin brother. The building was now only eroded, sand-blown wall sections with their tops melted down over the years by hundreds of cloudbursts. The cottonwood poles, and the ocotillo and reed roof they supported, were long ago scavenged or burned in campfires, but the memories there were good, and he had many spirits to visit in the dreams he expected to come in the moonlight's silver glow among blue-gray shadows in a town of ghosts.

The sun had already found the Cactus Man when he awoke in the dust of the roofless ruin. In his life he had never slept until the sun found him. He had always awakened before it could even find the tops of the mountains.

Vagabundo stood over him, waiting for the words which would place this curious happening in the past. The Cactus Man sat up and felt weak and tired. He had not slept on his bedroll or even used it as a pillow. "Where was I, " he asked the burro. "I do not think I have been sleeping. I was in another place. It had no dark or light or spirits, or place for me or spirits to be." The last thing he remembered from the day before was saying to Vagabundo, "The sun goes to find some others now," as the orange ball set distorted on the horizon.

They were the words Vagabundo had expected, but from those words at sunset till now, the burro had been distressed by the man's unfamiliar behavior.

The Cactus Man found himself too weak to stand without grasping the top of a section of fallen wall and pulling himself up.

“Something is going on with my body,” he told Vagabundo. “I do not think I can walk to Lajitas.”

He slowly made his way to the pile of canteens below the pack saddle setting upon an adobe stalagmite. He took a long drink of water, then poured oats into the pie pan. He wanted to make his meetings and he decided that the best thing to do was to try to get to the highway, a mile away, flag down a car heading toward Lajitas, and ask the driver to leave a message to Margaret, his cactus buyer, and to drop off the film and camera gear so Gene could pick it up.

He struggled to lift the packsaddle, but, finally, had it secured to Vagabundo, who was munching oats from the pie pan. He placed the camping gear and bags of cactuses onto it, and hung the canteens and camera over the ears of its frame. Then, without a breakfast fire, they started out. When the man put on the sunglasses, Vagabundo felt like events were returning to normal, and the burro began to relax.

Clinging to Vagabundo, he moved slowly across the almost flat terrain sloping toward the highway. It was ten a.m. when they arrived at the highway's edge. The Cactus man, still weak, but feeling stronger, stood by Vagabundo, who now was sure that the man was ill. The burro stood motionless in the heat radiating from the asphalt as he worried about his friend. The Cactus Man was not concerned about dying, but he was worried that he might not be capable of making the journey to fall into his grave.

It was fifteen minutes before a vehicle came along. The occupant was a woman who knew both of the two standing beside the road. Residents of the area, understanding its terrible and dangerous vastness, would always stop when someone was standing beside a lonely stretch of road, because the person could be in a life threatening situation. She pulled over and stopped to say hello and find out if there were any problems. The Cactus Man had not signaled for her to stop. He had been standing with his head lowered and his eyes shut, feeling weak and lightheaded, and he had not seen the pickup, which was now backing toward him.

The woman exited her truck and saw

that the Cactus Man looked tired. She asked if he needed any help as she supported his free arm. He looked at her face as though he did not recognize her. The woman looked into his eyes and understood that he was in distress.

"It's me, Nancy, I've talked with you at the Lajitas store. Remember? We talked there just two months ago."

The Cactus Man replied, "I am not feeling too good. I need to get to Lajitas. . . supposed to meet some people."

"I'll be glad to take you. But do you want me to take you back to Study Butte? If you're sick, maybe you should go to Study Butte and see about getting some help."

"No, I will be okay for Lajitas. I have some cactus on my burro, and some cameras for a bugman. Can you take all of us to Lajitas?"

"All but the burro. My truck can't haul him."

The Cactus Man weakly replied, "He will go home when I tell him. We can get him across the road, then I will tell him to go."

The woman, with as much help as the Cactus Man could give, took the bags off the packsaddle and placed them into the bed of her pickup. Then she helped him lead the burro across the highway where he slapped Vagabundo on the rump and said, "Go home, Vagabundo, go home."

The burro, carrying the packsaddle and camping gear and canteens, trotted along the roadside then headed southeast toward Terlingua Creek and the Rattlesnake Mountains.

Nancy and the Cactus Man arrived at the Lajitas general store fifteen minutes later and just before noon. Nancy helped him put the bags of Cactus under the ocotillo roof of a small patio outside the store. While the Cactus Man sat in a wooden chair in the shade, Nancy brought him a soda from the beat-up, red, coke box setting outside the store's sagging screen door.

"Lupe is minding the store today. I told her to keep an eye on you, and that you were expecting some people. I won't be back over this way for awhile, but I'll stop back by and ask about you. I have to go now. If you start to feel bad, call Lupe. Okay?" She patted the Cactus Man on the shoulder and departed.

The girl running the store opened the screen door, looked out at him, smiled, and yelled out, “Como esta, Juan Pablo? Need anything, just call me.”

He sat in the shade with a breeze from the Rio Grande cooling his face. He was not thinking about anything until he started to wonder why his usually buzzing mind was not thinking about anything. Then he thought that when life bites you, you have to bite it back.

He was thinking about what he could bite when the girl came out of the store and handed him a taco. “You look hungry,” she said. If you want more, just yell,” and she went back inside the store. The Cactus Man, with a little trouble swallowing, ate the taco and finished the soda, then dozed-off sitting in the chair.

As he slumbered a car drove up to the store, and the woman passenger jumped out and approached him. She snapped a couple of photos of what she thought to be a lazy old Mexican wearing bizarre sunglasses and returned to the car, which had the engine still running, and jumped in. The impatient driver, her husband, sped out of the driveway, making a cloud of dust which drifted over the Cactus Man, causing him to open his eyes and think that a dust devil had just passed. He closed his eyes and dozed again.

He was awakened by Margaret. While she tried to stir him, she heard him mumble something about having to fall into his grave so he could lie next to someone. "Juan Pablo, where is Vagabundo," he heard her say as he became aware? "Are you okay," she asked. "Just a minute, let me take your pulse."

Margaret, who had been an army nurse in Korea, now ran a plant nursery near El Paso, specializing in cactus. She felt Juan Pablo's forehead and checked his pulse, then she pinched the flesh on his arm to see if he was dehydrated. "You seem okay," she said. "How do you feel? Talk to me, Juan Pablo. Take off your Lolitas so I can see how your eyes look."

"I feel not to good, but better than this morning. I slept last night where there should have been many dreams. But I slept like a rock. No dreams at all."

"I don't see your burro, is he around someplace?"

Cactus Man, seeming more alert, answered her question, “I sent him home. That is where I need to go. Oh, yes, your cactus. It is here somewhere I put it.” He replaced his Lolitas and looked about. “It is here,” he said as he put his hand on a bag by his chair.

“Can I help you? Can I drive you home?”

“No thank you. There is no road. I have to walk. At least from the highway.” He peered into the distance for a few seconds, then laughed and said, “I never cleared my driveway. The rocks in it are elephants, but they act like rocks. I better not have a driveway because the park rangers will find my home. Is your home hidden from the rangers?”

“No, I don't believe that rangers are looking for either of us.”

She questioned him about his dreamless sleeping, and had him explain what had happened that morning. She decided that the old man had suffered a stroke sometime the evening before. “You need plenty of water,” she told him. “I'll be right back with some.”

Margaret was in the store when Gene arrived and parked close to the Cactus Man. "See you made it here," he said through his open window as he killed the engine.

Margaret arrived with a glass of ice water as Gene was standing by Juan Pablo. She handed the glass to Juan Pablo who stood up slowly and walked to the center of the patio and looked out across the river.

Margaret and Gene introduced themselves, asked each other to use their given names, and Gene told her about his encounter with the Cactus Man four days earlier.

She told him, "The Cactus Man is Juan Pablo, but to strangers he introduces himself as Cactus Man. Locals who have known him for awhile refer to him as Juan Pablo, but I've been told that he had a twin brother and their names were Juan Narcisso Luna and Pablo Isarius Luna, and that when his twin died he began to call himself Juan Pablo."

While the two spoke, Juan Pablo returned and sat in the chair. He began searching his pockets for the roll of film. He was just about to forget what he was searching for when his fingers found the film can.

"Here," he extended his arm to Gene, "here is your bug pictures—the pecas. Now we will both know the pecas. Show them to Margaret, she likes bugs. Oh yes, your camera and lenses."

"I see them. They're by your chair," Gene interrupted, "Don't worry."

Juan Pablo drank the water, stood up, and declared, "Thank you. Now, I must get to my home."

Margaret and Gene decided that Juan Pablo should be taken to the hospital in Alpine, and they told him that Gene would give him a ride. But, Juan Pablo was insistent about going home. He said he would never go to any hospital and that he had to watch after Vagabundo. He became somber when he said that more important than whether he lived or died, was where he died, and that must not be away from his grave. He had become so aggravated and emotional about it that Margaret whispered to Gene that it was best, under the circumstances, to try to get him to his house. She said she thought it was somewhere close to Study Butte or Terlingua, but she didn't know its location.

Gene agreed to take Juan Pablo home. That way, since he would be in the Big Bend for two more weeks, he would know where Juan Pablo was, and he could drop by and check on him a few times.

Margaret paid Juan Pablo for the cactus, hugged him, handed him four empty canvas bags, and placed the bags of cactus in her car. She gave Gene her business card, told him to call her in El Paso if he needed to, then she drove away. Glancing back with a worried look, she headed toward Presidio. She was wondering if the old man would be at the store next time they were supposed to meet.

CHAPTER 5

This is Gene Hart speaking. I'll take up the story at this point.

After buying Juan Pablo some groceries in the Study Butte store, we drove toward the western boundary of the national park. At the luckily unoccupied check point just inside the park's western boundary, Juan Pablo asked me to take a right turn onto the dirt road which led southwest to Terlingua Abajo and the tail of Santa Helena Canyon. After three miles, he said to take a right fork. I turned right and was on a rocky, rutted, even more primitive road. I put the truck into four wheel drive and we continued a half mile where the road turned due south for about a third of a mile, then turned and ran due north again and continued beyond a park boundary sign. Soon we passed the ruins of Willow. He told me that he and his brother had worked there at a candelilla wax rendering plant when they were young men.

We stopped just past Willow. He told

me that he lived a short trip from the road. Then he said that only three people had ever known the location of his home, and he made me take an oath never to tell anyone else. I placed the groceries inside the canvas bags and carried them, a small backpack, and my full canteen, heading south between Terlingua Creek and the lower slopes of the Rattlesnake Mountains to our left.

After a short hike, the Cactus Man began to move up slope into an area which seemed to lead to a dead end where steep rock faces would halt our journey. I looked around and saw no evidence of a building among the large rocks between the narrowing, steep walls of the ravine. Still moving upward, avoiding sharp, lechuguilla tips and walking around large chunks of fallen rock, we approached an impenetrable patch of prickly pear cactus and turned to the right. I followed him along the lower boundary of the cactus patch, ducking under overhanging pads, then, after turning around to see where we had come from, I looked again in the direction we were walking. Juan Pablo had disappeared. I continued on and arrived at a vertical face of igneous rock which halted my progress. I looked to my left and saw a narrow tunnel-like pathway leading upward again between igneous walls and under menacing overhanging cactus which formed a roof over the path. Thirty feet up the cactus tunnel Juan Pablo was waiting for me and saying that we were almost there.

We made our way between the cliff and under the cactus, and then turned to the right at another place where a way to continue was not apparent until your were upon it. Now we were on a tennis court sized, flat area with the outside rimmed by rocks the size of elephants, which isolated the area from view below. Above us, continuing up the mountain, were cliffs which blocked any view of the higher elevations.

Vagabundo appeared from behind a rock which was shaped like half of a dome, and which appeared to buttress the vertical rock face which extended above the flat area we walked upon. As I got closer to the dome, I noticed that it was built of many rocks, shaped to fit tightly together. I followed Juan Pablo around the sixteen foot wide structure to a wooden door set in a wall of mortar and stone, all the elements of which were the color of the surrounding scene and impossible to see if you were not directly in front of the entrance. This was his home, so well camouflaged that I had to stare at it to even see that it was a manmade structure.

"Mi casa es su casa," he said as he opened the door. "I build it when I was young and strong and had time to fit close rocks."

I went down seven steps into comfortably cool air. Under the dome-shaped rock masonry ceiling was a rough hewn wooden table with three crude but sturdy chairs on a floor of tightly fit flagstone. A hewn wooden bed frame supporting a swaybacked mattress set in the right side of the space, and a large mesquite-wood hutch with thick doors set inline with the head of the bed.

Cactus Man shut the bottom section of the entry door. Only then did I see that it was a Dutch-style door. The door faced southwest and gave enough light to see clearly inside, even though there were no windows. The back wall, which was the solid stone of the mountain, had what appeared to be a cave entrance. I approached the opening and saw no floor, but as I stood at the narrow opening, I saw stone steps leading down a curving passageway into the depths of the mountain. I asked, “Do you have a cellar? Do the stairs lead to another room?”

“If you will forgive me for being a poor host? Please, I must lay down a moment. You go explore. Take a kerosene lamp, the one with the reflector on the table will do. There is matches on the table. And, por favor, take one of the water buckets with you if you would be so kind. They are by the top of the stairs. Go look down the steps and you will be amazed. I will rest till you return.”

Juan Pablo lay down and I lit the lamp and moved to the top of the steps. They were steep, like a ship's ladder, and went beyond the light and curved downward into darkness. I could feel a cool draft as I began down the stairway which followed a natural chimney-like crevice which, in places, had tool marks where it had been widened enough for a man to pass through. Descending, I tilted the light upward to reveal a cleft that narrowed into shadow. The steps were stones set in mortar to span the rift they were built across, and a run of eight wooden steps spanned a crevasse. I reached the last step on that part of the stairway which was above water, and I saw steps continuing down into a pool. But, with only the dim light of the kerosene lamp, I couldn't tell how many more steps, or how deep the water. I was about thirty feet below the room above and inside what seemed to be a volcanic vent or tube. I raised the light to reveal a cavern twelve feet across, with walls ranging in color from burnt sienna to dark orange ochers. The pool was the chamber's floor, and the water touched the walls all the way around leaving no place to stand or walk except the last dry step, which extended to the right to become the spillway of a mortared rock dam in front of a narrow, open space. A thin stream of water flowed over the flagstone dam and poured silently downward. Peering down into the hole, I saw no bottom, and I heard no sounds of splashing below. I dipped the bucket into the pool, and returned up the steps, excited to hear the story about how this all had come to be.

Juan Pablo was still on his bed. I set the bucket of water on a stool by a small table holding a basin. I decided to let the old man sleep, but I didn't want to leave without asking him about how he had found this place. And, I was interested in asking if I could return and search for water beetles in the pool below. I glanced around the room for a book to read. There were none in sight, so I got some research notes from my pack and sat at the table. I also felt that I should keep an eye on the him to make sure he kept breathing and would wake up.

It was late afternoon when he said to me, "You are still here. I am such a bad host to go to bed with a guest here. Please forgive me."

The old man sat up on the edge of the bed, and just as I was about to ask about the tunnel and the stairs, he suddenly began to say that he heard voices and must get to his grave. Then, he fell forward onto the floor. I helped him back onto the bed. He pushed hard against me, trying to stand up. I asked him to calm down. He had strength in his left arm, but his right arm and leg seemed to be paralyzed. He relaxed and looked into my eyes and asked me to throw him into his grave if he died. He said he was dying and would be dead in the next few moments.

I let him stand up and he started for the door, but his right leg didn't move and I caught him as he began to fall. I assured him that I would get him into his grave if he died, then I persuaded him to lie back down on the bed.

I had concluded that he was having a stroke caused by a blood clot. His blood was probably too thick most of the time as he wandered with limited water around the arid countryside. Got to be clots, I thought, as I got a tin of aspirin from my pack, and poured a cup of water. I went to him and asked if he could swallow.

He replied, "I have always been able, before. I think."

"Try some water and see if you can swallow," I told him.

He held the cup with his left hand, drank it down, then said, " I can swallow, no problem."

I gave him two aspirin with another full cup of water. I placed the cup, refilled, by his bed, and he seemed to make a rapid recovery.

"I think I can get up now." He stood up

by the bed and I saw that some control had returned to his right side. I had opened the bottom of the entry door while he rested, and when he noticed it he said, "You better shut the bottom before she comes in and hides. It's the time of day she comes to visit. The hour before the sun leaves us."

I asked who 'she' was, and he told me to wait, and that I would probably meet her if I would be so kind as to come outside to see his grave. He was strong enough to walk, favoring his weakened right leg, and we went out the door, shutting the bottom behind us.

We moved to the area beyond the entrance, farther away from the trail in, and we stopped where a hole was dug. I saw how it was that a man who lived alone in isolation had planned to bury himself in his own grave when the time came, if, at that time, he had enough remaining strength and consciousness to do so. Along the side of the hole, and hanging partly over it, there was a pile of dirt sufficient to fill it. The dirt, looking like rich garden soil, was held in place by a wall of boards. The board dam was held in place by a single, slender, wooden pole that braced it to the other side of the hole in such a way that when someone fell in, they would fall across the brace, breaking it, causing the dam to give way and spill the pile of dirt over them. Beyond the hole an inscribed stone marker read, "Juan Pablo Luna" and to the right of the bury-yourself resting spot were two stone markers. The one next to the open grave read, "Consuelo Alvarez," below which the single word, "Angel," was inscribed. The marker on the right also read, " Juan Pablo Luna."

I stood there by him and spoke, "You're an amazing man. But, I don't think it's time to throw yourself into this grave."

"No. But the time is coming when I will lie next to Consuelo, with my brother on her other side, and the three of us will be spirits together again in this place." He turned toward the setting sun and said, "Come with me to watch the sun go to find others to torment or comfort." He pointed to a place between the elephant-sized rocks where we could watch a few scattered stratus clouds turn gold and orange.

As we sat down, overlooking the dry bed of Terlingua Creek in the distance, the sun touched the skyline north of Lajitas, and the April air began to chill. The sun quenched itself, and a cooling breeze felt refreshing, contrasted to the heat stored in the rock ledge I sat upon.

"Here she comes." I turned away from the vista and looked to see whom Juan Pablo was referring to. I expected to see a ghost or a person, but I saw a five foot rattlesnake crawling slowly toward us across the ledge.

"Do not fear our companion. She comes out to have the heat in this stone when the air becomes cold. She will not care that we are here. She is an old snake. I remember her as a small thing, only a foot long. We have watched the sunset together for years. I grew older, she grew longer."

The snake stretched out to her full length only three feet from us. I was poised to bolt, but then I relaxed and alternately watched the oranging sky and the basking snake, which appeared to be composed, and acquiescent about my presence.

Juan Pablo continued to speak, "Once when she was about three feet long, she crawled over and sat next to me with her body touching my leg. She watched me while I ate supper— some beans. I offered a spoonful to her and her tongue came near to the beans but she did not take them. She and me sat together until it was almost too dark to see, then she crawled into my lap. It was dark when she finally crawled away toward the cactus garden. The next night she watched the sunset with me, but never since that one time has she ever come to touch me again. I have wondered why. Did I smell bad? Was the bowl of beans not to her taste? Maybe she decided I was not worth knowing. . . maybe she just wanted to see what I was or tell me she would not bite me."

The air had shed the day's heat when we walked back to the dome. I opened the lower door which kept the rattlers out, and shut it behind us. The old man said, "You see why I have two pieces of door. I would not want to get up in the dark and step on her in my floor. She could bite before she thought."

Juan Pablo went to his bed and sat down. "I am feeling not too good again," he said weakly. I got another aspirin and a cup of water and offered them to him. He said, "I think I am soon leaving this body. I know what kind of plant we will be and I wonder, then, what animal or bug will eat us, then who will eat them, and if our spirits are one spirit or three who stay together. Sometimes in dreams I remember being a coyote and a something that flew, maybe a moth or a bird or a bee, but I never remember being a plant. Once, in a stand of Spanish Daggers, I buried my feet in wet sand during a rain storm, and I stood quietly and let no thoughts enter my mind. The cloud and its thunder moved away and the sun found me being a plant. My eyes were closed because plants do not have eyes. I stood there for hours until I think I lost time. I found time again when I hit the ground. I looked at my feet and ankles, and found I had grown no roots. No wonder I fell over. I do not think plants have any fun, but they are alive, and are many times the first homes of the dead. I do not think I remember anything while I am a plant next time again. Maybe so, or not."

"So, that's why you hauled the rich soil up here to fill your grave. So a plant will grow there with deep roots to find you and your brother and Consuelo Alvarez."

"I pull up the plants which have tried to grow above Consuelo and Juan Pablo so we can all become a single plant, and be as one. I keep a little mesquite tree on top in the dirt, so that when it falls, the deep roots will find us and bring us up. Fate will determine who we become someday after that."

"Fate has it in store for you to be together again with Consuelo and your brother?"

"Fate has never spoken to me. . . has told nothing to me, awake or in dreams. More than once I have dreamed of a spirit who knows Fate. The spirit said that Fate seldom even speaks to himself because he is not sure what will happen next. Fate has all of us and everything, but he does not know where he is going. He just moves along and things happen to him, and ruin his plans." He stopped talking and began to laugh. Trying to speak through his laughter, he finally got out the words, "Fate does not even know his own fate. He is a dealer who never knows the next card."

I began to laugh and replied, "He can't even make plans for the possible, because sometimes the impossible seems to come out of nowhere."

"What you said," the Cactus Man laughed, and we both laughed until I thought it could be harmful to the old man's condition. I told him that laughing so hard could cause him to have a serious attack. He replied, "You mean I could die laughing? Ha, ha, ha, what a thing better could happen than to fall into my grave as I die laughing?"

With those words his face seemed to turn the color of mixed red and brown, and we both laughed even harder.

It was dark when I realized that I had not brought a flashlight. Juan Pablo had lit a candle setting inside of an empty sardine can, and it set on the table. He seemed to be acting normally as he walked around the table. His legs and arms were functioning.

I said, "I seem to have left my flashlight in the truck," and waited for his reply.

"The trail is dangerous at night and hard to follow. There is the moon, but I have no lights other than candles and kerosene. A cot is folded behind the cabinet. You can spend the night here if that is not asking too much. If you feel you cannot stay the night, I will guide you back to your truck."

I had nowhere to be that evening, or in the morning for that matter, and I certainly didn't want a stroke victim walking along cliff edges in the moonlight, so I thanked him for his hospitality and said I would be pleased to accept the invitation.

"Good," the old man happily replied. "We can fix some supper, then I would like to show you my bean collection, and maybe you can do me the favor of writing some things down for me, if you would be so kind. Some words about the beans."

"I'd be glad to help in any way I can. You saved my life the other day, and I owe you more favors than one. If you want, I'll take you into Alpine for a checkup with a doctor I know there. I'm sure he can help you with your attacks, and don't worry, I'll pay him. What do you think? I owe you at least that much. . . and more."

"I am 80 years old and have riches beyond belief and never been to a doctor. The medicines seem to be doing all I need. They are giving me time to tell someone who might write the stories about my beans. That is all I want to do before I die. But first, I fix something to eat."

CHAPTER 6

After a meal of sardine tacos eaten by the light of one candle, Cactus Man began to clear the table. I offered to help, but he asked me to remain seated. He then placed two kerosene lamps on the table and lit them. He stood across the table from me, supporting himself on the back of his chair, the lamps casting two looming shadows of him, curving up the wall and onto the ceiling.

He began to speak, "I have asked them, but never been told what spirits do when a person was not thinking of them, or dreaming of them. None of them ever revealed anything except that they thought they dwelled in plants when they rested. They told me that some things are not for the living to understand, because there are no words to explain a placeless place where time is ever flowing but not moving. I think maybe it is true that spirits only come back from their plant eternity when they are thought about, and can have the feeling of time moving again when the living have a dream, or go to places like dreams. At other times spirits may not be dead, but unthought, in a plant or, for the short time needed for passing thru, in an animal or person that ate the plant, but always needing the strength of a living person to call them forth, out of their resting place. But, maybe, they can all float into a same place and have a fiesta anytime. I do not know. I do not think they know much about that other world when they are not in it."

Juan Pablo stopped talking and walked to the entry door and looked out onto the moonlit mountains of rock, then returned to where he had been standing.

He continued to speak, "Forgive me, but I must tell you these things before you can understand the beans. When Juan Pablo died, I thought back on our life together. That is when I knew my memories had become weak and were going away, or becoming not true, maybe making real the way things could have been. I felt a duty to those who I had known in life. A duty to keep their spirits alive by remembering, but there was many days and years gone from me."

"I was wondering about those missing years one night while I sat at this table, as usual, cleaning pinto beans before I put them into a pot of water to soak overnight. I was sorting little rocks and little dirts from them, when I see a bean with the face of the orphan, Lupe Navato, who had worked at the Hot Springs trading post for Maggy Smith, who had the store. I had not seen Lupe in many years, but looking at the bean I could see her at the store. Lupe had a very round head, so round that she had no chin or cheeks or nose that stuck out too far. Her face looked like a ball with her face painted on it. I had never looked closely at the colorings on pinto beans before, but for a long time I looked at that bean. After a while, I did not see the table or the lamp and I forgot the feeling of my body, and saw only the bean, then it was not a bean, and memories returned of Lupe Navato. Memories I had forgotten. She appeared in the place I was, but I was not with my body or in this room. She was longing for any news, and to know if Maria Lago had a baby boy or girl. I knew Maria Lago and I was sad to tell her that she had died many years ago. Then she said, 'That is not possible, I talked with Maria as her baby was ready to be born. Only just before I flew like a bird with Maggy Smith, who held my hand and talked with me.' "

"I ask her how she got here. She said she thought she lived in a cactus and came from places where people are reading a book, and that the book is always open to a page where her name is, and when they turn the page, she is where someone else reads the page with her name on it. Once, she said, she came to be by a child when the father was reading the page aloud, and it was a story of her coming to the trading post and her job there. She said that people do not see her and that she likes to be read about when someone is out of doors so she can enjoy running and playing."

"The thought came to me that she was in a plant until Maria Lago had called her, or Maggy Smith dreamed her, or until I had thought of her, or the reading of her page brought her, then, I was suddenly back at this table and Lupe Navato was back in her plant, or someone was reading her page. Since that night, for twelve years, I look for beans which made lost memories come back to me, and I now have many spirits to visit with when I dream or stare for a longtime at a bean until I forget my body is with me. Now, let me show you my beans."

He went to the hutch and returned to the table with a tray holding small tins and bottles. They clattered as he set the tray on the table and said, "These are my diary. It is not words on paper, but the drawings which the bean plants put on their children. Before I began to look for the ones which tell me something, no telling how many memories I cooked and lost. I must tell you, I never learned to read and write too good, but since I found out that the spirits of the dead come to time from a plant, to live by thoughts about them, I have tried to learn to read better, but I am too old for it. Oh, I can write many words, but they come to mean nothing, and no one would read them. Now, while I am alive, I look at each of these beans and go into the past and people appear to me and we talk and go places, but I am not long to be among the living. So that is why I am asking you to write the stories I tell you about these beans."

"Out here people are few, and many have had to die alone. But we knew everybody who lived here. We have been to their houses, ate with them, heard their stories, buried many of them. Now some of them stay in plants. They know that much, but when I ask them what they do there, they do not seem to remember, but they remember their visits with me, and their life as a person. I question them many times about what they do now, but their memories are worse than mine, much worse, like they have none at all. So, if you write stories about them, and make a book for people to read, I will be very grateful. And for payment I will give you a map showing the way to places where you will find things you can sell for a great amount of money."

I looked into his pleading eyes and saw his concern for the lives of the spirits he thought he brought to life again, and I felt how desperate he was to have them continue to materialize from the ethereal limbo he feared they existed in when they weren't being remembered.

I was prepared to write all night when I said, "You don't need to pay me anything."

I was glad to help the Cactus Man. Hell, I was still glad to be alive and not being shredded by buzzards and coyotes or sun dried into jerky in the Solitario.

He replied, “You will please accept my maps to my cosas antiguas. They could not be found for years unless you go to them. They would be safe with you. I know that, somehow.”

Then, speaking as he got up, he went to the hutch. Standing there, he said, “I must give them to you now. I might not be able to when I am dead. Maybe, but maybe not.”

He slid a board forward on the side of the hutch and pulled a bundle of folded papers from a shallow compartment. “I do not feel like myself,” he said, as he pushed the board back into place. He turned toward the table, “I hope to be alive long enough to tell the stories of all my beans.”

He sat back down and pushed the bundle of papers over to me. I didn't reach for them and they set where he had pushed them.

He continued speaking, “Some of the stuff from the days of the Spaniards you can think about giving to museums. Sell the gold and silver coins, and jewelry. You need new truck tires. I saw that. And please, please help me to fall into my grave if I die while you are here. Are you ready to begin?"

I said that I would help him. He watched my face a moment, then looked down at the tray and touched several tins, the kind which once held salve or snuff or pills. He selected one and held it up close to a lamp. I could see the year 1900 scratched across its lid.

"I'm trusting everyone to your care," he solemnly said.

"This one I will tell you about next, but we can start with this one," he picked up another tin and returned the1900 tin to the tray.

The tin he opened had no date on it; just two rusted eyes scratched on a green enameled lid across the brand name— 'Kalb's Unguent.'

I got the two, new notebooks from my pack, opened one and took pencil in hand. "I'm ready to write," I said, expecting to hear mundane chronologies about people who lived boring, day-to-day lives in this uneventful part of the U.S. I wasn't a religious person. I had never seen a spirit, but I knew I understood delusion and hallucination were real at times, they had been for me, and the Cactus Man, living alone for such a long time, could probably conjure hallucinations with the drop of a hat. I also knew the man who had saved me from sure death was kindly and caring and only as eccentric as I would have expected him to be. I pushed the bundle out of the way of my tablet as I thought about the junk the Cactus Man must have accumulated in stashes all over the place throughout his cactus collecting routes. He opened the lid and slid six pinto beans onto the table.

CHAPTER 7

He showed me a bean as he spoke, and he began to tell the story of his bean diary. I began to write the story of each bean. The following is my narrated account of the bean diaries revealed by the Cactus Man that evening:

These beans remind me of our days as little boys. One has a figure of our mother, and one has the hat our father wore. And this one is of our little house, where we were born, and the cornfield which set just to the north of the Rio Grande and close to Boquillas. Our father spoke English, which he made us practice and talk to the Gringos, and he was a boss at the mines for awhile. I remember most my father talking with our corn. He told us that the corn said that our family was everything that they, the corn, wanted to be. He said that while we laughed and moved about and played, all the corn watched us and grew big and sweet so we would eat them and make them apart of our lives. . . and we did.

He put down a bean and picked up another.

This bean was foretold by my mother one night in my dreams. She came with her mother, and her grandmother and her mother. They said that I would find a bean which would show all the family for many generations, and the next day I found this bean.

I leaned forward to look closer, and I saw a pattern across the bean which looked like a line of human figures holding hands. I told him that it was a very unusual bean.

Cactus Man said, See the people? They are the ones they told me about. The oldest mother said we came from a tribe called the Jumanos, and that they were from the ancient people who first lived along the river where it made the big bend. She told me how our family had long ago avoided the Spaniards, and how they went into the mountains each year to hide when the Comanches would come at the end of summer. Then my youngest mother said other people came and went, but our family had survived. They were proud that we were Indians, and not Spanish or Mexican or Gringo. The old mother said that I had the ways which would keep me safe from the Mexicans and Comanches. I like visits from my mother spirits.

He picked up another bean and continued talking.

And on this little house bean is a hill which our father and us sat by one cool day, shucking corn, when we saw a rock leave its place and roll down beside us. Our father said the rock wanted to come down and rest; that it was tired of clinging to the side of the hill. That afternoon my brother and I put the rock back in its place and it stayed. My brother and I had discussed the idea that rocks have minds, and we decided that they did not know where they were and could never feel tired, or feel anything. We felt sorry that it had rolled down from where it had always been, so we put it back. We felt sorrow for it and at the same time knew it had no feelings. Sometimes I think that we just did not want anything to change around us. We liked our place the way we had come to know it, and every rock and cactus had its place in our minds.

As we grew older we found that things

change no matter what we did, or how many rocks we returned to their place. We could see that the people of the Big Bend age and die, and the things they make become worn away into piles of rubble like Presidio San Vicente, because some of these things had occurred in our lifetimes. We felt that the mountains and desert went on forever, though. Then, when we were about twenty-five years old we met a geologist. We called him the Rock Man. Look at this bean, it reminds me of him because this shape looks like the hammer he carried to dig out and break rocks. We had English to speak with him and he asked us to guide him around to any unusual rocks or places we knew. So we did and he paid us. We learned something from him which changed us. He said that even the entire Big Bend changes, and that it will only be a desert with mountains for a blink of an eye in the story of the world. He said the entire Big Bend was once the bottom of a vast sea that was here for a longer time than it will be as a desert, and he showed us shells of sea creatures which could be found in the layers of white rock all around our feet. After the land was water, it was once a land of fire and melted rock from deep in the earth, and he showed us which rocks were once red hot and flowed like water. We believed him and had dreams of the land we lived in as once covered by water, and then a place of lakes and shores, then fire and ash, and then a forest which would become mountains and desert. We thought how short our lives were, because we would only know it as a desert, and we would come and go before it made itself into something else. Now that I am old enough to know that people need the land to not move and flood and burn, I am glad that I can walk the same mountains and canyons, because they are a part of who I am. Sometimes, to this day, when I come upon a rock that has recently rolled down from its place, I will carry it back up and replace the unthinking rock, and slow down the blink of time's eye as it sees the story of the Big Bend.

This last bean has crosses and a man with a severe face. It calls me back to the times the priests and the missionaries came to our house and tried to convert my mother and father to Christianity. They would all tell our father that he was doomed to an everlasting torture called Hell if he died unconverted. The Protestant Christians told us that we would burn in their Hell if we were not their kind of Christians, and the Catholic Christians told us that Protestants would burn in their Hell because they were not of the true faith.

Our father would listen to them, and then tell them that he did not want to be a part of any belief that was so vengeful, and he did not know any Indians believing in the spirit world, who thought that a good and kind person of any religion would die and go to eternal torment.

Our father believed in an afterlife as a spirit, and that good, dead people had spirits who had a joyous spirit life and lived in plants and could even be reborn when a woman ate the plant while with child. He said that bad, dead people were spirits who lived in piles of dung until they had done enough good deeds to undo the evil they had caused in life. He believed that evil doers' spirits worked their way up from dung to plants before they could be a part of the thoughts of the living.

Our father accused the Christian visitors

of having a cruel view of life, and many times told them as they departed our house that they would no doubt die to dwell in cow manure until they quit telling good people to be what they demanded or face eternal torture.

As for animals, he believed their spirits went into other animals— sometimes their own kind and sometimes into other kinds of animals and even bugs. Our father had accounted for everything including bad dreams, which he said were caused by Christian spirits trying to prove to us that they were truthful about Hell, and if we were not Christians, their spirits would make a Hell, and try to put us in it. After a while they quit coming to our house. We were glad to be rid of the hateful priest with a severe face.

Cactus Man placed the six beans back in their tin and told me he could not recall much more about his younger days, except that his parents kept the old ways and never converted to Christianity.

He reached for the 1900 tin and emptied two beans.

"Nineteen hundred was a year the world was supposed to end. This bean has that year on it."

The Cactus Man held the bean up to the light and I could see 1900 appearing in a legible pattern of broken, lightning-shaped lines, followed by what could be construed to be an exclamation mark. Then, holding up the second bean, he showed me patterns of human figures running about wildly, like a cave drawing, or something in a museum of modern art.

He continued telling the stories and I continued writing:

We were 13 years old in 1899 when we first learned that the Christians among us thought that the world ended every so often, especially on meaningful dates like the end of centuries. It was a time of fear and activity among the people. Many of them thought that Christ was coming at midnight when the year became 1900. Others thought the end would come at dawn the following morning when an angel would blow a horn. There was praying and crying and preparation among the faithful.

All the week before the end of everything, at the shrine of the Holy Virgin in Boquillas, people were crawling on their knees and kneeling and confessing sins and seeking absolution. Those that could, traveled to see a priest in Boquillas Del Carmen, the village in Mexico.

Then, two days before the end of all of our earthly lives, a man shouted that the old palapa holding the shrine was an insult to the Virgin, and they must build her a new shrine, not a palapa, but an adobe with sturdy walls and a new roof before the end came. If not, he said they would all be damned to Hell.

The local adobe brick maker protested, but soon people were carrying away his bricks to a high hill close to the village, and closer to Heaven. From the very old to the youngest, everybody who could carry a brick worked day and night with a passion. I must confess, all the excitement and fear affected my brother and me, and before we knew it, we were hauling adobe and mud up the hill. My father and mother seemed to stay very relaxed. They calmly sold tamales to the workers. Our parents asked us why the believers who were going to paradise were so upset.

On the night before the end came, everybody had worked so hard and long to get the Virgin's statue into its new shrine that most people slept through the sunrise at the end of their mortal life. My brother and me stood around the shrine till noon then went home, and all the faithful who had prepared for paradise seemed relieved to be in the bitter cold of a north wind that came to the Big Bend in the afternoon. The cantina was full of people that night, and all the beer and mescal was consumed in laughter and music and gone by the next day as everybody celebrated not going to paradise. My parents and the others of the old ways thought it all very silly behavior.

By my watch it was nine o'clock when the 1900 beans went back into the tin. I asked the cactus Man if we could take a break. He said we needed a pot of coffee. He went to the stove, put in some grass kindling and prepared to heat the coffee water. I walked to the entry door and stood there looking up at the black sky and the universe of stars.

“It's okay to go out now,” I heard the Cactus Man say. “Open the door and go out for fresh air if you wish. She is hunting down in the cactus patch. It is too cold for her up here now. I water the cactus and throw scraps of food into it which mice and rats grow fat on, and she hunts them."

I went out and stood in the cold, star-filled night. An occasional breeze came, and, as each was passing, it felt like the Milky Way was spinning down and swirling around me, and I felt as if I were divine in nature. I laughed at myself for feeling majestic, a galactic immortal, when just a few days before I was a fool without water, dying, dehydrated by the nearest of those stars. I smelled coffee and the stellar swirl magically retreated light years.

With feelings of my fragile mortality I returned back inside the rock house, still warmed by the day's heat stored in its thick walls. I sat down in front of a cup of coffee and three non-dairy creamers and some cubes of sugar. I tore open a creamer and streamed and stirred a dissolving, spiral galaxy of white into the blackness while the Cactus Man spoke of a milk goat he once had years ago when he lived in Terlingua Abaja. He added that the goat was not a good listener

CHAPTER 8

While I sipped coffee, Cactus Man removed another container, a small jar, from a shelf in the hutch. He sat down across the table from me and pondered the jar, set it down, had a sip of coffee, and then unscrewed the lid. He slid three beans onto the table—the only beans in the jar.

He continued, "These three beans are Consuelo Alvarez, my brother, and me. Oh, no, no, no. These beans are three miners I knew in Terlingua long ago. The 1940's war. I think you will be interested when I tell you their story. They deserve to be remembered. They were kind and gentle, but were cursed by bad luck."

I saw a kangaroo rat hop to the edge of the shelf of the hutch, as Cactus Man spoke. I told him that he had a visitor behind his right shoulder.

Then as he turned to look, the little animal jumped two feet through the air to land on Cactus Man's right shoulder. The visitor nuzzled the man's ear as if greeting him, then it ran down his arm and onto the table, and tore off a piece of tortilla from one remaining in a saucer. It jumped back onto the hutch and ran to a topless, match box in which it took a seat and began munching tortilla while glancing back and forth at Cactus Man and me.

"A house pet," he said. "She joined up with us a few years ago. I will go ahead and quickly tell the story of the three brothers who came to work the mines because 'Sweetie Pie,' that is the mouses name, listens to that story from beginning to end every time I tell it. That has made me believe she maybe has eaten a plant that held the spirit of one of the brothers. Maybe spirits can live in mice."

He poured the three beans onto the table. He sorted out the three beans and showed me a Jose bean and the two beans representing Jesus and Carlos.

Cactus Man continued the tale of the unlucky brothers: They came to the quicksilver mines happy to have work. In just weeks after arriving they had all been killed in different accidents. Unbelievable, strange accidents. Things fell on them. One was killed when a burro fell on top of him. A timber fell on the head of another, and the third was killed in a hail storm when a big chunk of ice, bigger than the other hail, hit him as everybody was running for cover. We buried them all in the Terlingua cemetery.

Then, soon after the third unlucky brother was buried, some of Terlingua saw a bright light, and all of Terlingua heard a thunderous sound. The next day a hole was found blasted into the graveyard next to their graves. It was eight feet across, and as deep.

People thought things would continue to try to fall on the brothers. The town decided it would be good to dig up their coffins and bury them a safe distance from the cemetery, because people were afraid something would fall on them while visiting relative's graves if the brothers were buried there.

Cactus Man finished the story, then said, “I would tell you more about them. . . but maybe that is all I remember.”

I noticed that Sweetie Pie had fallen to sleep on her back in the match box. Her long, back legs were sticking up in the air and her long tuft-tipped tail was close to her hands which still held bits of tortilla.

Cactus Man got up and went back to the hutch. “Here we are,” he stated, “This is the jar we are in.” As he spoke he returned the jar of luckless miner beans to a shelf and withdrew a similar small jar and removed the lid. He slid its three beans onto the table. “Look,” said Cactus Man, “one of us is facing up, and so is Consuelo. I don't know which of the two brother beans is me. I may surely already be in the grave next to Consuelo.”

I asked, “May I turn the third bean?”

“Yes, go ahead.”

I picked up a card from an old, worn deck of Bicycle playing cards which had set fanned out, faces up on the table. The queen of diamonds and a two-eyed jack watched me as I purposely withdrew the three of clubs to turn over the third bean. On it was an identical face design as on the other, brother bean. I thought about how it should be that no two beans, like snowflakes, could possibly be duplicates, but here in front of me were two identical beans. I stared at them and began to see subtle differences, like the differences one sees in mood or demeanor in the faces of identical twins. The faces were the same, but one seemed more serious in temperament, and somewhat less capable of sympathy. I used the card to shift the beans, and, in a new position in light and shadow, the beans seemed to switch emotional characteristics. What had been the serious bean now had a placid expression, and the other appeared almost sinister. I pushed the beans closer to the light of a lamp, and their expressions both appeared to become comical.

As I stared at the beans I began to realize that I was becoming too involved with pinto bean personalities, however, the patterns were intriguing because of their mutability, as changeable in appearance as the Man in the Moon, so I inspected them a bit longer, then I looked up at the eyes of Cactus Man and saw him looking intently at the Consuelo bean.

We sat there a moment longer, then he spoke, "I never found a bean that did justice to her beauty. This one came the closest."

I joined Cactus Man in gazing at the Consuelo bean. It looked very much like a quick-sketch artist's drawing of a young

Elizabeth Taylor with a face framed by tresses which reached to her breasts. Above the bean-designed portrait were cloud-like forms—a turbulent sky which extended the full length of the bean.

He spoke, "If you feel like writing the story of rest of my beans, now, I feel strong enough to tell it. I do not feel so well, so if you do not mind, I would like to begin. It is a long story."

I told him to begin when he was ready.

"Oh, yes. First I must get all the people of this story. There are many more beans. I need to remember them all."

Cactus Man went to the hutch and opened a drawer and returned to the table with a clay jar. He sat, removed its lid, and pulled out a mitten-sized cloth bag with a drawstring. He fumbled with the string, loosened it, and poured about two dozen pintos onto the table.

He spoke, while I continued taking notes; writing down as much as I could of his words.

"I know all these beans. I knew all the good people and villains whose spirits were somehow drawn by these beans upon themselves. I do not know how it happened to be, but I think maybe pieces of the air the people breathed out was breathed in by the plants which made these beans, and that explains why everyone and every animal seems to have a pinto bean somewhere with their face on it. The air we breathe out must someday blow into every bean field in the world."

I watched as Cactus Man arranged the beans. He placed them in rows and gathered some in groups. I tried to notice if there was a design that by chance resembled me or anyone I knew, but the beans had patterns which only the Cactus Man understood. One bean pattern was, however, obviously a mustachioed hombre wearing a classical Mexican sombrero. In any orientation or light the hombre's mouth would purvey a marked sneer.

With the array of characters assembled and sorted, the Cactus Man glanced up at me and began his tale again:

I have looked at these beans many times. But, I was alone here at this table when they told me their story. Myself, I just let the memories come and live without words. I have tried not to think things which did not happen, and at times I had to stop myself when I would begin to imagine things which would have given their story a better ending. Things which would have given better lives and less suffering, but I would stop myself and return to the memories of what had been the truth of the things that happened. A spirit sitting at this table once told me that my wishing could not change the present ways of the spirits who were once the people of these beans.

When I am in bed though, and the beans are put away, I think of the way things could have been if there had not been evil men, and Fate had been always good, and could know that his goodness would follow his wishes. That he could know the next card in his deck, and not turn it over if it was bad. Just cut to the next good card. It has always seemed to me that in such a harsh land as this, where people do the same simple things to stay alive, where there is not much going on. . .just the sun and moon, the mountains and the desert. . . that here, Fate could have each day and know the next. How could Fate not know what is to happen here? I think men complicate things for him, when under a full moon simple life can go loco, and then people can do crazy, unnatural things which he cannot plan for.

CHAPTER 9

Cactus Man looked at the beans and pushed one to the center of the table. He said, "This bean shows the day that Consuelo Alvarez lost her mother and father and brother. It was the autumn of 1915."

I looked at the bean. There were three sets of patterns which could, with a little imagination, appear as three prostrate figures.

He continued speaking; beginning a heroic tale of luck and magic and faith, and a tragic tale of death:

Consuelo Alvarez was a zagala. In English it means a young woman who herds the goats. She and her goats were at a spring about a mile south from the adobe where she lived with her father and mother and younger brother. The family lived south of the Rio Grande, upriver from Boquillas. Her father worked at the mines and farmed a field close to the river where the ground flooded each spring. Their house was back from the river, behind a little rise.

On that day Consuelo heard guns, but she remembered her father's words. They told her to never go toward gunfire. To run the other direction and hide. It sounded like it was coming from by her home, so she did not know what to do. First she turned around and went back toward the spring, then, worried about her family, she turned and ran along the trail to her home.

She arrived just as a gang of bandits rode away. She found her father shot dead outside the adobe. Inside she found her mother and brother, both shot. Her mother was still alive, but dying.

She said to Consuelo, Forgive me my child, I think I am leaving you.

She died in the arms of her daughter.

Maybe you will not understand what I tell you now. You see, death in this land was a frequent visitor in those times. Life was so hard that people here made much of life—weddings, births, holiday fiestas—and little of death, because it came often. Consuelo had already seen an older sister die from sickness. Her grandmother and grandfather had both died close by, and she had been to many burials. Death was a part of her life, but Consuelo had always seen death from natural causes, and she wanted to know what kind of man would kill her family. She wanted to know why such a man did not believe the teachings of the Blessed Virgin.

She was standing by her father's body when some neighbors appeared. The men had guns. The women rushed to Consuelo's side to comfort her.

Consuelo's family was buried the next day, close by their adobe, along the trail to their spring. Consuelo was expected to go live with her mother's brother. He lived in Boquillas with a wife and four children, but Consuelo vanished. People looked for her, but she was not to be found.

My brother and me knew nothing of what had happened to the Alvarez family. We knew the father well. We had worked beside him for the quicksilver mine on the Mexican side, and we had last seen him and his wife and children at the store on the Texas side on Cinco de Mayo in Boquillas.

When the bandits killed them, we were

returning from Marathon, driving a team of mules pulling an empty ore wagon back to Boquillas. We were probably close to Persimmon Gap, about thirty-five miles north when it happened.

Everybody seemed to know who did the killings. There were many bad men in those days, but one was a bloodthirsty outcast who led a band of men. They usually rode far south of the Big Bend country, deeper in Mexico, but his fame had spread north. It was said that he had killed his brother and many others, and his name, all we had ever heard him called was, El Viboro—which means something. The viper in Spanish is called La Vibora. So, I suppose El Viboro meant a man viper.

My brother and me arrived in Boquillas the day the family was buried. Many people went to the funeral, and many searched for Consuelo Alvarez. We got supplies and soon left town to go up Juniper Canyon to look for the meteor that was said to have crashed to earth there. We planned to get pieces of it and sell them, so we took four burros with us to carry a load out of the canyon.

The day we left Boquillas we made it to

Glenn Spring. It was a village, then. We passed the night with a cousin who lived there. People said someone had seen a woman walk by, a distance from the village. Too far away to see her face, and nobody saw any goats with her. She was going up toward the canyon, and that was the last they saw of her. We told them we would watch for her while we traveled. Only our cousin knew we were looking for the meteor.

Next morning we set off. Word was that the meteor had come from the heavens, so we thought it might have gold. We were excited about it, but we did not know exactly where to find it. Once we were in the canyon we went slow and looked along the bottom and in the little side canyons. We searched all day and found nothing and made camp in the dark.

Next morning we pushed further into the canyon, looking everywhere. Then, in the dry bed of the creek, in sand, we found recent footprints. Small feet. Too small to be those of a very big person. They were barefoot. We followed them to a place where the person had put on sandals, and we followed the prints, losing them in rocks. We thought surely they were those of the woman seen going toward the canyon. All day we climbed further up, following the creek bed while we looked on both sides for the meteor, and expecting to find a person. We found nothing and nobody.

We were close to the head of the canyon. It was narrower and the walls steeper, and the creek bed had places which would be waterfalls in time of rain. We worked our way along ledges and kept looking. The area was rugged and steep. We climbed over piles of rocks that had fallen from high up the sides, but by then we had talked ourselves into gold fever, and we were sure the meteor was worth a fortune. We kept climbing, looking at every unusual rock. It was a year later that we were told that meteors were mostly iron with no gold, and not easily broken to pieces by a pickaxe.

It was afternoon when we saw a figure climbing up the mountain making the south side of the canyon. It seemed a woman or a child wearing a white robe. We yelled out and she turned and looked at us, then she continued climbing. We decided that the person was possibly a child, and maybe someone who was crazy. So we thought to go help them come back from the dangerous climb.

We climbed after them. Our calls echoed and echoed off the mountain sides. We began to wait after each word so that the many voices in the air would die away, and the person would know what we said. We spoke in Spanish.

After a while of climbing as fast as possible we were just several hundred feet below them, and we could see that the person was a young woman.

Then, suddenly, the wind changed direction and began blowing down into the canyon from the north, coming over the mountains and dropping on us. This new strong wind carried a cloud of dust it had gathered in the desert. Soon, even close as we were to her, the dust hid her from us, but we kept climbing in golden light where there were no shadows.

We stood close below a ledge when we saw her again. She was on the edge, maybe fifteen feet above.

We watched as she raised her hands to heaven and heard her say in Spanish, "God, I cannot climb to the top of this mountain and be closer to you. You must hear me from this place. I ask why you let my family die at the hands of a bad man? My father. My mother. My brother."

We knew at that moment that it was the daughter of Jesus Alvarez, and a moment later we knew that God had listened to her, for suddenly her long hair reached up toward Heaven, and the shawl on her shoulders rose up on each side of her and became the wings of an angel. We looked at the miracle with anxious joy filling our chests, and amazement flowing from our eyes.

For a few seconds we saw an angel on this earth, then, above the top of the pine tree behind her, a small light appeared and began to grow. It became a ball of white fire and grew bigger. Its intense light cut through the veil of dust. Then the ball of white fire lifted for a moment, and then began floating down.

The angel's hair came back down, and her wings became, again, just a shawl draped over her shoulders. The light from the ball lit the air, and the air became oranger and then redder as its light penetrated out into the dust.

As this light from God settled to the ground behind Consuelo Alvarez, her body, with arms now stretched out straight, cast the shadow of the Cross out though the dust, and the Cross grew taller as the ball floated down and touched the earth, where, with a sound like water being poured into a frying pan of hot grease, it sank out of sight. We climbed rapidly up to where she stood, unmoving, except her lips which said, "Oh Blessed Virgin, I heard your words."

The dust was now thicker in the air, and we helped her place a bandana over her mouth and nose, then we did the same. We could not see as far as five paces when we began to descend to the place we had tied the burros.

No words were spoken as we worked our way down. Consuelo Alvarez seemed to be in a state of grace. She stepped without looking down at the ground. She seemed to float beside us.

As for my brother and me, we suddenly had more religion than we had the day before nineteen-hundred when we were covered with sweat-streaked mud in our desperate attempt to soothe the temper of the Blessed Virgin with a new shrine, before the horn blew us to heaven.

We camped where we had tied the burros. The dust was gone by the time night had been upon us for two hours. We made a fire and a special meal of tortillas and stewed jerky for Consuelo Alvarez. We thought she was a saint and a messenger of God.

She would not lift her hand to eat or drink when we offered the food to her. She just looked out into the darkness. We waited for her to speak or do something. We knew that saints all had a message or did great works and miracles, but she was silent.

Finally we placed a cup of water onto her lips and she drank some of it. We then made a broth and placed it to her mouth and tilted it. She put her hands around the cup and fed herself.

It was a moonless night. We made a bed for her and kept the fire going, waiting for her to lie down or speak, but she did not. We had just built-up the fire when we decided to roll a cigarette. As we puffed it, the little breeze changed direction and carried a cigarette smoke onto the face of Consuelo Alvarez. The smoke hurt her eyes, and for the first time since she had held her cup of broth, she moved and wiped a tear from her eye. It was a pain we gave which I have always remembered, and a pain I will never forget.

We came to sleep sitting by the fire, and we awoke before the sky began to lighten. The fire was almost out, and Consuelo Alvarez was asleep in the blanket we had placed by her. We sat in silence so we would not wake her. One of us placed twigs on the fire so we could see her beautiful angelic face.

Too soon, the sky came to light, and she stood up. She moaned a sweet sound as she stretched her arms upward, while rising erect on the tips of her toes. We watched with anticipation, fully expecting her to keep rising. But, she lowered her arms, fluffed her long hair, turned toward us. We saw a faint smile come and go on a sad face.

"I must go to find the man who killed my family," she said, looking right at us. "The fire on the mountain last night was the Holy Virgin. She told me to forgive the man and tell him of salvation through confession."

We told her that we saw God's fire, also, and we swore to help her. "But, should not we eat first?" we asked her. "It is a tiring trip back to Boquillas."

"While I slept, the Blessed Virgin told me, again, to find the man and save his soul and make him a man of God. She did not tell me to eat."

She began walking down the creek bed. We shouted after her, "Did she tell you to die of thirst and go unconscious from hunger? Surely, she knows that to find the man, you must be alive."

She paused, then walked back and said that she would prepare a breakfast for us. While she cooked, we decided that she was truly on a mission from God, and that God placed us at the scene of the miracle to tell us we were meant to aid her.

We ate and drank, then loaded one burro. We insisted that Consuelo Alvarez ride upon a burro. After all, a blessed child on a holy journey, ordained by the fires of heaven, should not have to walk in worn-out sandals.

We worked our way out of the upper, difficult to traverse reaches of Juniper Canyon, and by noon we were where the path was over worn trails winding around hillocks and between lechuguilla, ocotillo, and cactuses, all the way down to the Rio.

CHAPTER 10

The Cactus Man looked at me and said, “To continue the story of the beans, I could use a bit of coffee. How about you?”

I agreed, and while he built a small fire of twigs and grass in the little stove, I went to the door and peered out into the night. The moon was behind the cliffs above the dome , but still high in the sky. My watch said 11 p.m. I peered into the shadows and wondered if the rattler was close by.

“Our coffee is hot. Come and fix your cream and sugar.”

I returned to my seat, and as I prepared my coffee the Cactus Man dug through a dark green tin box he had placed on the table. He then held up a photograph, looked at it a moment, then turned it so I could see.

Holding it close to a lamp he said, “Look. It is a picture of Consuelo Alvarez, and that is me and my brother standing by her.”

The picture was of three standing people posing for a camera. Cactus Man and his brother stood with Consuelo between them. The brothers wore loose-fitting, white pants and white, pull-over shirts, and sombreros. The girl was as tall as the men's shoulders. She had high cheek bones and long, black hair. She was wearing a simple white dress which draped over her thin body like it had been made from a flour sack. All three were wearing sandals, all three appeared quite dusty and tired, without smiles, but just bland expressions with squinting eyes caused by the photographer having placed them facing the sun.

Cactus Man said, “I am the last person on this earth who knew her. Perhaps there is someone who saw her pass by, or maybe heard her voice, or knew how brave she was. But I think those people have all died.”

Looking at the photo I asked, “Which is you?”

He looked at the photo and replied, “ I do not know.”

Then, Cactus Man began to speak at length, and I took notes again. He continued:

It has been many years. I remember this day. We had just found her two days before this picture, and were on our way to find the bandits who had killed her family. We had just come to the store on the north side of the Rio Grande at Boquillas. But, I do not know which brother is me. Juan Pablo and me spent our lives together, and now I do not remember if I am my brother or me. I could be dead and not know it. We worked for the mines, harvested candelilla, lived in the same adobes, herded cows. We shared our lives, and I know I am Juan Pablo, but I do not know which one.

Maybe I chose to be the brother who lived. This would be a cruel thing to do to a brother, but if I did this terrible thing— to take his remaining years—I only do it so I can tend the grave of Consuelo Alvarez, and my brother beside her. Life is hard here and sometimes you have to find a way to live through thirst, and heat or cold, and keep going, for if you look back, the sun will catch you, and you will not survive this place. Sometimes you can have to be the one who did not die. To live to keep a promise. To live until your spirit is purified. Maybe, to just survive. A man can have more than one reason to live.

Cactus Man quit speaking. I sipped the last bit of coffee in my now cold cup.

He fished another photo from the tin box, and holding it for me to see, said, "This is me and Consuelo by our casa near Castolon."

I saw a young Cactus Man wearing boots and dark clothing, and beside him was a beautiful young woman.

He said, "This picture was made in 1918. It was a big year for the end of a war. I remember. And it was the end of the grasses and the cottonwood trees. Cattle had eaten all the grasses, and the mines and candelilla vats had burned most of the trees. But, I remember before when the Big Bend country was prairie and trees that were not only in the Chisos in the high country. All the soil washed away after that, and the land has been this way since then. Dryer every year."

I sympathized and asked, "Do you feel up to finishing your story about your search for the bandits. I'm curious to know what happens."

He returned the photos to the tin box and placed it into the hutch and sat down and, as I made notes, he returned to his narrative:

By now everyone knew Consuelo Alvarez was seeking El Viboro to save his soul. We had stopped at Glenn Springs on the first day of our journey out of Juniper Canyon. People there knew that she had lost her family, and Consuelo told them what the Virgin had told her to do. From there the word spread up and down the Rio Grande. My brother and me were in her service. We had no choice after the appearance of the holy light and the vision of Consuelo as an angel. For us it was help her or burn in either the Protestant or Catholic Hell.

That night in Glenn Springs, while Consuelo slept, we talked with our cousin. He said it was sure death to search for and find El Viboro and his band of murderers. We told him what we had seen—the light of God. He crossed himself and agreed that he too would feel compelled to aid her if he had seen what we described.

We went to bed feeling we had no choice and wishing that we had not sworn to help her. Now we either accompanied Consuelo, a messenger of the Holy Virgin, or be condemned to Hell. We considered telling her that the Virgin had told us that she was to go to the house of her uncle and wait there for further instructions. Would a lie to save all of us be so sinful?

The last argument of the night was again which Hell we would go to—the Catholic or the Protestant? We wondered how many Hells there were, and if we might have to go to all of them. We went to sleep without being so sure God, Christ, the Holy Ghost, and the Virgin, all together, could protect us from El Viboro. They did not protect the Alvarez family.

In Boquillas we learned that El Viboro was close by, in Mexico. An old man and woman told us that they recently had to escape from the bandits who had camped where they lived—southeast of Mariscal Mountain, which lay up river. They told us where El Viboro was just two days ago.

We listened to their story and they told us how to get there. While they spoke, some children outside the store asked Consuelo Alvarez to play with them. It was the first time we saw her smile and heard her laugh. Then the man with the camera arrived and insisted that everybody pose for pictures.

After that we headed to San Vicente to cross the river into Mexico and save the souls of the bandits.

Two burros were loaded and all three of us had to walk. We had food, much water, and extra blankets for the colder autumn nights. The way had no trail and was mostly unfamiliar to us, and was rough going, so we had to slowly make our way. Consuelo wanted to walk fast and seemed determined. We were glad there was no moon, so she could not have us travel at night. Sometimes we lost the trail and had to backtrack, but late afternoon of the third day we heard shooting ahead of us, and as we got closer we heard men shouting and laughing.

We pleaded with Consuelo that we should not interrupt a family party or a wedding. We were fearful that we had at last found El Viboro. A secret from Consuelo was that we had decided it was best if we never found El Viboro, and we hoped that she would tire of searching. We had lost our nerve and feared for our lives, and, just as much, for the life of Consuelo Alvarez.

It was then, as we stood just out of sight of the laughter, that Consuelo's sandal, which had been repaired twice, came away from her foot as her step fell onto a piece of broken, whiskey bottle. Blood poured out, and while we bandaged it, a man came around the hillock which had been hiding us. He was very drunk and looked at us and staggered and fell, then got to his feet and began to piss on a cactus and onto his boots. While he pissed he asked us if we had seen his horse. While trying and then giving-up buttoning his fly, he told us, "Come and join the party. El Viboro is going to shoot a goat with his new shotguns." The man staggered a few feet then fell over and onto a prickly pear cactus. Consuelo asked us to help move him off the cactus, and we did. He cussed us as we lifted him and laid him onto the earth. He moaned and passed-out or died. We did not know which. His belly was breathing and his eyes were a little open, but only white showed in them.

All of us stood around him, then we heard another pistol. We told Consuelo, "This is a bad time to try to save their souls. Surely, it was the Virgin who kept that man from returning to tell them we were here."

We watched as she limped to a burro and removed the load. We thought she had come to her senses. That she was going to mount the burro and ride away with us following as fast as we could travel. We told her, "The Virgin will help us find the bandits when they are sober and their souls are available for salvation."

Then, just as on the day we saw the fires of God bless her, our chests filled with anxiety, this time without the joy, and amazement flowed from our eyes as we watched Consuelo, atop the burro, bring the head of the animal toward the bandit camp and gently heel him forward.

We had to join her. Shame for thinking about not doing so was already washing over us and mixing with dread and fear until we felt like we were drowning in hot soup.

Stunned, we looked at each other and said, "Goodbye, brother," and joined Consuelo and walked on either side of the burro.

The party got quieter and quieter as more of the bandits saw us. Finally, all were silent. Some of them had wide-open mouths as though they could not believe the sight. We moved slowly through the parting crowd toward a man holding a shotgun to the belly of a tethered goat. Consuelo stopped the burro in front of the man, who looked at us and smiled, then without looking away from us, discharged both barrels of the gun into the side of the goat's belly while his big teeth kept looking at us.

He turned to see the effect of the blasts and said, “See, I told you. I can butcher and clean the carcass at the same time with my short-barreled scatter gun. Who doubted it? Who owes me money, now?”

There was a murmur among the men, then Consuelo's sweet, clear voice announced to the big teeth setting below eyes coldly scanning the group of swaying bandits, “The Holy Virgin has sent me to tell you to go to confession and you will be forgiven for killing my family.”

We nervously began to back her story, “My brother and I were there. We saw the light of the. . .”

The man holding the shotgun interrupted, “Shut up, you idiots,” then he stared at Consuelo for a considerable time.

All were silent, then, finally, one shouted, "Viva El Viboro!" All began to shout "Viva!" and an old man began to play a guitar and the gang began to swig whiskey.

Two men grabbed each of us, and a fifth man lifted Consuelo from the burro, then we were forced inside the adobe El Viboro had entered.

They stood us in front of a table which El Viboro sat behind. "I am such a lucky man," he said, "to have such an opportunity. Are you related? Is this your daughter? Sister? Wife? Speak up!"

We told him, "We are traveling with her. To help her find you. It is said that you killed her family. She has been told by God and the Virgin to come and save your soul. We were there. We saw the fire come from heaven when she was told this."

El Viboro replied, "The Virgin sent you here. Well, that means she sent you to me, and I will send you to her, after we enjoy your company for the evening."

He then ordered his men to tie us, which they did, and then they pushed us onto the dirt floor. We sat there while he told the men who tied us to go outside.

Consuelo still stood in front of him when he said, “El Gallo, listen,” and then he whispered to the remaining bandit, who quickly departed and shut the door behind him.

The whispered secret was not secret for long, for then we heard El Gallo say loudly to the drunken men outside, “ El Viboro is now screwing the girl while her men have to see her pumped, then he will shoot them with his new shotguns. He is going to blow off all the legs of the two men with one shot, then blow off all the heads of the two men with one shot. Hey! Who was supposed to skin the goat? Well do it. I am hungry. Then El Viboro is going to fuck the woman again until he gives her to me. Then, after me, all will have her. But keep her alive. El Viboro wants her returned with a beating heart.”

We heard a cheer go up and the music continued. Consuelo began to say something to El Viboro, but he stood up and told her to keep quiet. She kept talking, anyway, “You have killed many but it is not too late to save your soul.”

She kept on talking as he pushed her chest onto the table and lifted her dress, then ripped it away from her body. She was naked and still talking about his salvation when he went to his new shotguns leaning against a stack of wooden shelves in the corner, close to where we sat tied-up. He lifted one gun, opened the breech, and then closed it and set it back in place in front the other matching gun.

Consuelo had grabbed her torn dress from the floor and stood clutching it over herself. El Viboro tore it from her hands and stared at her body. He pulled her hands away from covering her breasts and vagina.

Grasping her hands he spoke, " You are older than I thought. You are already a woman. Good. Children die easy. Too easy. Not much squirming, and little begging and pleading for life. Mothers plead and cry for the child, but the child does little. It is a challenge; more fun to kill men. They run at my guns with their machetes. Pow! My smoke blows them off their feet. One misfire and I could be hacked. I like to let them run just up to me. I take the chance. Women and children are no real pleasure to shoot. I do not know why I do it. You shoot me, senorita, and you all get to leave here. You say you have come to save me. I think you want to kill me. Let us see."

El Viboro turned and faced us, then he lunged quickly at us and raised his hands and shouted, "Boo."

As he did so, we startled and bumped the shelf which supported the two guns at its other end, and with our heads turned to the side, expecting to be kicked, we saw the shotguns slide to the right, with the barrels of the second gun now resting in front of the gun El Viboro had just handled.

"Let us see how holy you are senorita," he said as he picked up the front gun and walked to Consuelo. "Take the gun." Consuelo stood motionless. "I said, take the gun."

He went to her and placed the gun into her arms. "Hold it like you are going to use it," he demanded, then he put the stock against her shoulder and placed her finger on the front trigger. He then sat down at the table. "So pull the trigger," he said.

He wanted to hear the click and know

she was not sent by God to save his soul. He needed to know that she wanted to kill him; that she would pull the trigger.

We were frozen, watching the scene, seeing the thin naked body of the young Consuelo looking so fragile and yet, still calm.

She finally spoke, “I came to save your soul. I still am here to save your soul. Will you not listen to one who was sent to you by the Virgin herself?”

One of us, my brother or me shouted, “Shoot him, Consuelo.”

“Yes, shoot me Consuelo. They know what God wants you to do. . .or maybe, the Devil.”

El Viboro touched the end of the barrel so that the gun was pointing at his stomach. Consuelo was silent and unmoved.

“Pull the trigger senorita. Surely you can squeeze the trigger. . . . No? Well then, give me the gun.”

El Viboro knew the gun was empty. He knew it was the gun which he had just checked and placed in front of the other. That crafty, cunning, murderous El Viboro was sure the shotgun the girl held had killed and blasted-out the guts of a goat, and was not loaded, so he reached forward and grabbed it and pulled it toward him to take it out of Consuelo's hands.

The gun came toward him, but Consuelo's unthinking finger on the front trigger did not, and instantly, in a blast of noise and white smoke, the innards of El Viboro were on the wall and he was cleaned and killed with one shot. Consuelo stood dazed and wide-eyed.

Outside, a drunken man yelled, "There went all their legs," and the other members of the gang roared with laughter and shouting.

The man who was El Viboro's lieutenant walked toward the wooden door to the adobe. Inside, we were frantically trying to untie each other. Consuelo, in shock, stood facing the red and brown splattered wall, still holding the double-barrel shotgun. Coming to her senses enough to begin realizing what had occurred, she could not suffer looking at the dead man and the stained wall, so she turned her back to the scene and was now facing the entry, and still holding the gun with her finger unmoved from inside the trigger housing and against the second trigger.

El Gallo came to the door, paused and said to the men outside, “I bet they are half the height they were,” then he entered the adobe to enjoy a scene of misery and suffering, but the door pushed against the muzzle of the gun and Consuelo fell backward. The butt of the gun came to the table’s edge, and this time the gun stopped and Consuelo's finger kept going as she fell backward.

A thundering blast of white smoke blew the door shut, and eight lead pellets removed El Gallo’s neck. His head occupied the space where his neck had been when his falling body came to rest, slumped against a wall.

Outside, the gang, those who were not already passed-out, shouted and laughed. The familiar voice said, “There went all of their heads.”

We had untied ourselves and had begun to think of how to get away. We took the gun from Consuelo and told her to be quiet. We checked the other gun and found it empty, and no shells were in sight.

On the back of the adobe there was one high little window. We decided we could get through it. We were all shaking, even

Consuelo. We moved the table over to the little window. We climbed onto it and looked out. No bandits were in sight and there was a mound we could get to and be quickly out of sight, and hopefully make our way back toward the Rio Grande.

We were just about to go out the window when we realized that Consuelo was as naked as a baby, and that she had nothing on her feet, except a bandage. We grabbed a pair of sandals off a shelf, and a man's shirt, then we heard a man outside at the party shout, "El Gallo, the goat is ready to cook. Come out. Save some of her for us, El Gallo."

We thought the shouting man might come in, so we quickly went out the window. One of us helped Consuelo to the ground. She was still naked. We quickly carried her through the cactus and thorns. She was still barefoot and her bandage was coming undone, with its loose end trailing just above the ground, but we dared not stop.

After about twenty minutes we were out of breath, but still moving, when the end of the bandage snagged on a cactus, pulled on Consuelo's foot, and caused us to stumble.

The entire bandage lay unraveled in the dirt—a white ribbon with a string of big, red spots on it. As we lay there, flies began to alight upon the open wound. We felt far enough away from the bandits to stop a moment. We tore a strip of cloth from the lower part of the shirt we had taken, then helped put the shirt over Consuelo. One of us supported her while the other bandaged the foot. We then adjusted the sandals to fit her small feet, and we took up our journey again; taking turns aiding Consuelo to walk and climb. We traveled off the trails, and went across arroyos and up and down the hills between them.

We were thankful we were not in the heat of summer, for it was almost night before we felt safe enough to stop at a barrel cactus to get some water. We had not seen or heard anyone since we escaped. We used a stone to smash the water-laden cactus and poured its juice into Consuelo's mouth, and then we drank. It was a big cactus, and we all were satisfied.

We went a little further and found a place out of the wind. We gathered some dry grass for bedding, and huddled together for warmth all through the night. A sliver of moon called the coyotes, and they answered with their song. The two of us only slept for minutes at a time. The crescent moon set early and we spent the cold night waking and sleeping in starlight. One side of us was cold, facing the night, and the other side of us was warmed by the sweet body of Consuelo, who lay between us, warmed, we hoped, by our bodies and the blanket of grass we had sprinkled over her.

CHAPTER 11

The Cactus Man quit talking. I looked up to see him staring at the beans. I asked, "Are you feeling okay?"

He didn't move or blink for fifteen, or so, seconds, then he placed two of the bandit beans into the cloth bag. During his tale he had shown me a bean which represented El Viboro and one which was the pictorial essence of El Gallo. Each bean had grown a pattern which appeared as acceptable variations of a Simon Legree.

He gathered eight remaining bandit beans and fished more beans from the bag. He inspected each one, returned some, then placed on the table one more bean next to the eight bandit beans.

He continued to slowly move the beans around, placing them in different groupings.

I asked, "Mind if I take a break?"

"Please," he replied. "Mi casa es su casa. I am seeming to have trouble remembering these beans. Maybe, fresh coffee."

"Don't interrupt yourself; allow me to make a pot. I need to move around a little, anyway," I replied.

At the stove, as I fixed the coffee, I commented on the ristras of dried red chilies, strung on sisal twine and hanging from nails on the side of the hutch. "Do you know any of these peppers? Are there any stories they tell to you?"

After a moment, he looked up from his work and then looked back at the beans. "No. Those are just red chilies. They never look like anyone. Do you see somebody in them? A spirit has never come to me from a chili pepper. I do not know why. Maybe in dreams after some very hot chilies."

We drank coffee, and I waited for the rest of the story. Were the bandits going to chase after them? Then, the cup slipped from his hands and split apart upon the table, spilling the bit of coffee remaining in it. He appeared frozen and seemed unable to move.

"Are you having an attack," I asked, as I went to stand beside him, lest he fall from his chair.

He finally placed his hands on the table and became less rigid. I grabbed a rag and mopped up the coffee. I dried each bean it had wetted, and returned each one back to its position.

I asked him if he needed to lie down, and he answered, "I feel I should continue. Maybe some bread. Would you be so kind as to get me a piece of bread and some water."

"Food would be good," I answered. "What if I open a can of Vienna sausage? Does that sound good?"

"Si. You must sustain yourself. I regret that I do not have more to offer you."

I made a sandwich for each of us. We ate without talking, then I offered him another aspirin, which he swallowed, then he began where he had stopped the story.

He continued:

The next part of the story of Consuelo Alvarez I must tell differently. I have mentioned that I sometimes do not know which brother I am. Our family often called us either name because we were identical. After Consuelo was taken—but that is a part of the story I must tell later—my brother and me built an adobe to live near Castolon. Soon after our casa was built, my brother, for the first time in our lives, moved away to dwell alone on the south of the river. He then lived in the abandoned adobe of the family of Consuelo Alvarez.

He became ill there, and I went to tend him. He died the first week, and his last words were to me. He said that he did not want to die, then he said something I could not believe. His eyes opened, he asked me to forgive him, then he looked at the ceiling and said, "God, I am Juan Luna. God, it is me, Juan Luna. Have mercy on me for stealing my brother's name. I am not Pablo." And he died just after that moment, with his finger pointing at me, and these last words, "You are Pablo Isarius Luna. Remember."

The year before, I had mostly thought I was Juan, because my brother had been calling himself, Pablo, most of the time. I was thinking that one of us knew which one of us he was.

After my brother's death, I was confused and returned to Castolon where I soon became ill. Day after day I lay in bed too weak to rise. The bed seemed vast like a big flat cloud which supported me without pushing against me. It was like I floated above it. I was the size of a mouse at the center, with the edges so far away that I knew I could not crawl to them.

While I floated there, crazed with fever, I heard a voice coming from someplace unseen. The words told me everything each of us had done, my brother or me, but, after the fever, I still did not know my deeds from my brother's, because the fever did not reveal which brother I was. Once it told me that I was Juan Luna, but, then, I remembered my brother saying he was Juan. There seemed to be no days or nights, and the voice told our story many times until I knew the next words to be spoken, and they began to come from inside me like I was reliving the first days after El Viboro was killed.

When I recovered, people in Castolon told me they had expected me to die. On the first morning without fever, I awoke wondering who I was—Juan Luna or Pablo Luna. It was making me crazy. I asked people who had known us. Some said I was one, and some the other. That is when people began to call me Juan Pablo. But, even today, when I awake from dreams of our days as children, I sometimes awake as somebody who saw us both in the dream.

Cactus Man then continued the narrative of the events of 1915, and began to speak of Juan and Pablo as though he had been a separate observer of both. He began to ramble and the events were no longer sequent. I could not discern whether it was a small stroke affecting him, or that he had become more emotional. He continued to speak and his thoughts slowly became organized again. As he spoke he placed beans and moved them around on the table as if they were actors in a play. As fitting the story, he would juxtapose the beans representing the characters about whom he spoke. At times he was animated. At other times his eyes moistened as he continued the story.

I wrote as he spoke; now with the understanding that his earlier comments about whether or not he was his brother were not a result of any current strokes affecting his memory, but this confusion about his identity was something from the distant past.

At one a.m. he said, "I am so happy. At last her story is being written. Now, Consuelo will have her spirit life to enjoy when people read your words about her. Did I tell all the story? Am I just dreaming it all one more time?"

I answered, "No, I don't think you have told all of her story. And I am sure this is real, and that you are here with me."

Then, Cactus Man tried to stand, but he collapsed back into his chair. I helped him as he tried again to stand. He seemed very tired, and how ill I didn't know. He looked about the room, turning his head as if searching for something, then he looked into my eyes, and asked, "Spirit, do you know who sleeps in my bed? I need my bed."

I supported him and directed him toward the bed. While beside it he said, "That is the bed of my brother. I am so tired, I hope he does not need it."

With those words he lay down, closed his eyes, and went to sleep. I stood over him for awhile to make sure he was breathing regularly. Then I gathered the diary beans which were on the table, and placed an empty drinking glass over them. I was fearful that Sweetie Pie, or some other creature, would make a meal of the unprotected beans, to nibble away no telling how many memories. I looked over at the hutch and saw that Sweetie Pie was yet asleep in her match box bed. Then, I checked again to be sure the Cactus Man was breathing. I glanced around the room. Everything seemed to be in order.

I turned my attention back to the story of the beans. Earlier, when speaking about events involving his brother, Cactus Man had always said, "We did this," or, "We did that," but he had completed the saga of Consuelo Alvarez by sometimes speaking about the brothers' actions as though he was an observer of both, quoting the words of both, and expressing the thoughts of, and reasons for, both brothers' behavior. He recalled actions which Juan had done, and actions which were accomplished by Pablo, all without revealing who he was now.

I thought about all that, and, with another cup of coffee, I returned to my seat at the table and read my notes of the story I had just been told; beginning with the first morning after the shotgun killed El Viboro and El Gallo. I paid attention to the pronouns he had spoken in an attempt to write the story the way he had told it, and to try to discern if there were any clues about which brother he was.

CHAPTER 12

While Cactus Man slept, I continued writing while his words and my notes were fresh in my mind:

Juan awoke the final time of that almost sleepless night next to the beautiful young woman he was pledged to assist and protect. He sat up and looked at her still sleeping. He looked at her sweet face, then his eyes moved down her body. Barely visible in the cold gray light of early dawn, for a fleeting moment, only partly awake, he thought he was looking at a tarantula. He was preparing to grab it and toss it into the cactus, then his mind cleared and he realized what he was seeing. It lay there like the back of a tiny black kitten, curled up and asleep, between her thighs.

The shirt had ridden up to her waist, her arms were folded tightly against her chest, and her hands were snuggled into her armpits. He moved his face close to hers. Did she look like a sleeping angel? He wondered if an angel could kill so easily. Close to her face, he saw an innocent child, but how so? Her breath smelled like roasting mutton, a sweet, succulent, enticing aroma. She stirred and drew her legs up into a tight fetal position, and the sleeping kitten nestled, no longer visible.

He imagined that her bare belly was that of a mother cat. He thought, she could be a cat. A cat could sleep so soundly after killing, but not an angel, or an innocent young woman. Perhaps she was an avenging angel, and, to protect her innocence and grace, the Virgin had not told her anything, but merely used her as the instrument of a just God delivering vengeance upon the wicked murderers. Possibly she was just out to kill the men who killed her family. But what about the light in the dust? Could not the Devil have a ball of fire? After all, the fire did burn itself into the earth. Possibly it burned its way back to Hell and into the Devil's arms.

Pablo awoke shortly after Juan. He saw that Consuelo, the messenger from God, was half naked in the cold, and he tugged upon the shirt, trying to cover more of the sleeping girl's bare legs. Consuelo, reaching without waking, also grabbed the tail of the shirt and pulled it over her knees and continued to sleep.

It was the coldest part of the desert night—just before the sun rises, when creatures began to hide from the sun to survive another day.

We were still on the Mexican side of the river, and close to it. We roused ourselves, and, without words, piled the tussocks of dry grass over the sleeping Consuelo.

Juan departed and returned after a time with another armload of grass stems, and blanketed it over her exposed feet and shins.

He whispered, "We must be quiet. For all the bandits know, you or me could have killed El Viboro. Surely they are searching for us." Pablo agreed with a nod. Juan continued, "I did not hear anything last night. They are probably somewhere on the trail. . . or sobering up, or yet drunk and still at their camp. If we could know they were riding out late, maybe we could make it to the river and cross. The closest crossing at San Vicente, or maybe at Solis. We can cross anywhere. We do not need a shallows."

Pablo replied, "Consuelo's foot must be

kept dry. It needs sewing. We need a crossing where we can carry her above the water."

We had slept on a mesa which was beside the seldom used, dead- end trail we had come in on from San Vicente crossing. The way down was crevices between cliffs above a steep talus slope of large broken rocks to the trail below, but it was dangerous to be on the trail with the bandits possibly searching for us.

We were deciding which way to go when Consuelo awakened. She stood up and asked, "Where are we? Are the souls of the bandits saved?" She turned around and looked into the distance in each direction. "How did I get here?"

We did not know that Consuelo Alvarez had not purposely pulled the triggers to kill two men. We did not understand that Consuelo remembered nothing but disconnected pieces of events since the first blast from the shotgun she had held. We thought she was a good shot and had the nerve to shoot El Viboro and El Gallo after she realized we three were going to be killed, no matter what.

She approached us and pleaded, "You

must help me find the bandits and I will tell them God's message and save their souls."

Juan sighed, "Not again. You have already saved two bandit souls. At least you sent them to death somewhere. The bandits will kill us on sight, now."

Consuelo remained quiet a moment. She looked at Pablo and asked, "What does your brother mean? Have I caused someone's death?"

He told her, "You were a part of something which came to pass, but I do not think you were the cause."

Juan, with accusation in his voice, looked at Pablo and said, "She held the gun. It was two direct shots. She killed them and they deserved to die."

She looked at Pablo and asked what we were talking about. "You were given a gun which you held when it killed two bandits," replied Pablo.

She answered him, "I have never fired a gun."

Pablo told her, "I saw what happened. You held the gun because the bandit chief placed it in your hands. Do you remember that? Do you remember yesterday?"

"I remember cutting my foot and the men who killed a goat. I remember standing naked when a crucifix was given to me. It was heavy and it jumped in my hands, then, through the smoke of a censer I saw the Virgin peer from behind a curtain and sign herself. Now I am here."

Juan, after seeing the naked Consuelo, had grown lustful. In his thoughts he was seeing Consuelo more as a young, beautiful woman, than a saint or angel. He began to tell himself that the ball of fire had returned to Hell and that Consuelo had not heard the Holy Virgin. He knew he wanted to make love to Consuelo, but he knew that he could not if she was on a holy mission.

Driven by desire, he began to speak not too kindly, "Then it can only be that God used you. He made the bandit place the gun in your hands, and then aimed it for you and used your finger to pull the triggers. All that while, you thought the gun you held was a crucifix. Does God use the innocent in such a way?"

Pablo was not defending God, he was defending Consuelo against the harsh tone of his brother's words when he told her, “God did not make you kill anybody. Those two idiots killed themselves. It was their fate. Fate killed them, not you Consuelo. The two dead men killed themselves. What they did, pulled the triggers.”

Juan looked at the ground. He had just realized that he only wanted to screw Consuelo. Guilt then poured over his desire.

Consuelo Alvarez was crying. She sobbed the words, “I must find their mothers and ask forgiveness, and I must find the other bandits and deliver the Virgin's message.”

Juan tried to ignore her words, and she continued to sob as he spoke, “They can backtrack the trail we walked with the burros, but they cannot follow our path to this spot. What if we headed upriver past Mariscal Canyon? It is rough country, no good for horses, but we could cross.”

Pablo added, “We have escaped them and now we must quickly find a way to the river and cross back to the north side. The other end of Mariscal is probably eight miles for a bird, but for us with no water, no food, and Consuelo's injured foot, we cannot do it.

Maybe we should sit here and watch the trail below, and hope the bandits will come and go. It would take us half an hour to get to the trail from here, and we would be visible the whole time. Tonight will be more moon. We can work our way to the trail then, and down to the river if the bandits come and go, or if they do not come at all."

Speak of the Devil and he comes, for at that moment the two burros, one still packing our gear, came into view about a quarter mile away where the trail vanished around the end of the mesa. They were heading toward the river.

We crouched down and pulled Consuelo down with us. Be quiet, we told her. The three of us watched the burros proceed at a fast, steady walk, and we brothers knew that burros walked so only if they were being driven. The animals had been in sight for only a couple of moments before the mounted bandits appeared behind them.

Consuelo stood up to shout at them, to tell them of her duty to deliver a message of salvation, but before she could open her mouth, Juan covered it with his hand and jerked her down, out of sight. Pablo, peering from between tall rocks, watched the burros pass below and walk out of sight; followed along the winding trail by the bandits, eight of them, all on horseback.

His hand still muting her, Juan spoke to Consuelo, "Angel of God, they think you are an angel of death, at the least. After you shot their leader and his lieutenant, do you not know that they hunt us to kill us. They would not now listen to a message from God. They would shoot us or worse. Violate you and drag all of us behind their horses."

We nervously waited, sweating out the last sweat our dry bodies could make. Then, we got low, even closer to the ground, as we heard a shot from the direction of the river and the bandits.

Consuelo did not flinch. She continued staring calmly and blankly at Juan who yet held a hand over her mouth, and an arm around her waist. He told her of how they had departed El Viboro's hideout and how we had taken the shirt so she would not be naked.

She watched his lips until he finished speaking, then she removed his hand from her mouth and looked down at the shirt. "I wear a bandit's shirt? Where is my dress?" Her questions were the only indication that she had understood or even heard his words.

Juan answered, "I think, El Viboro's. Not the one he wore when you placed him out of this world. It was on a shelf, folded and clean. He ripped apart your dress. I don't think he cares if you wear the shirt." Juan released her as he spoke.

Consuelo stood up. Then, on tiptoe to see below, peering down at the vacant trail asked, "The men who just rode by, were they the men of El Viboro? If they are, I must go to them and tell them the Holy Virgin has told me that they are forgiven for killing my family, but they must confess and repent."

Pablo told her, "Have you not heard us? They would not listen. They would be very happy to see you, but your words they would not hear."

Juan then said, "Get down! They are returning." We peered in the distance at the place where the trail from the river first came into sight. Again, Consuelo had to be held and muffled as the bandits rode past, now herding just the one loaded burro ahead of them. Juan asked if Pablo had counted eight returning bandits, and he answered, yes.

"We must be sure the bandits are not lurking," Juan said. He told Pablo to make his way to the end of the mesa, to a place where he could see the trail again, in the direction the bandits traveled. Pablo departed, moving rapidly, winding through the lecheguilla and cactus atop the mesa.

When he returned he saw Juan was still restraining Consuelo, pressing her body close to his and still holding his hand over her mouth. Pablo spoke, "They are a mile up the canyon and out of sight beyond a hill. They must be returning to their camp. Maybe to bury El Viboro and El Gallo. If we hurry, we can get across."

Juan released his grip on Consuelo. She stood and backed away from him while wiping her lips with her forearm. She turned to look at Pablo with an expression in her soft eyes appealing to him for help. He told her that for now she must avoid the bandits, and that they must all get to safety and decide, from the other side of the Rio Grande, how to save the souls of the bandits. Pablo assured her with what he knew in his mind, but not in his heart, was probably a lie, when he told her they would all return after resting and eating in Boquillas.

Without a look of disappointment, but just the same look of peace and determination, she allowed us to aid her down through the rocks and rubble. On the trail Juan and Pablo progressed furtively, rushing Consuelo along, and ducking behind any cover to glimpse the trail behind. We noticed bright red blood spreading on her bandage.

At the river we saw why the bandits had turned back. The Rio Grande was too swollen to cross, and the muddy, rushing waters washed around the bottoms of the cliffs above the only trail toward San Vicente. The autumn cold front, which had created the dust storm in which we had discovered Consuelo Alvarez, and saw her consecrated by the fire from heaven, had produced rain somewhere upstream on the Rio Grande or the Rio Conchos; too far away for the rain storm to be seen from the Big Bend country. And, just as it had many times in the past, the river had unexpectedly surged and continued to flow mightily on its road through an unrained on desert where the plants along the shores, just beyond the torrent, set in arid atmosphere, with their roots in dry sand.

We knew there was no way to tell how long it would be uncrossable. It could be a day, a week, and the bandits could return. We retreated and climbed a ways off the trail, far enough to not be seen or heard while talking about what we should do. We needed water and food.

As we discussed the situation, Consuelo sat quietly, then began to hum a lullaby and braid her hair. Both of us were amazed at her tranquility, then Pablo decided that one chosen by God would surely, upon realizing that as fact, would of course be at ease, no matter how dire her circumstance. After all, heaven awaited them. Paradise. What mere earthly fears could the anointed possibly have? As we both silently admired the serene Consuelo, we heard a voice call out from the trail.

"I must speak with you. You will surely help me. I beg you."

Taken by surprise, we hurriedly

hunkered down, forgetting to grab Consuelo, who stood up and answered the voice, "We will help you."

Pablo raised his head just enough to see. He watched a thin, older woman as she climbed toward us. Our other burro, wet, and with fresh mud caked on him up to his sides, followed her up.

"Hurry," Pablo said in a voice straining not to shout. "Hurry, before you are seen."

Juan had pulled Consuelo down, and again continued to restrain her while Pablo helped the woman into and behind the rocks which hid us from the trail. Our burro had halted part way up, and he had returned to the trail, and stood there.

The woman squatted among us and said, "Dios mio. Gracias, gracias. Que Dios te bendiga. Bless you. I followed you yesterday from the camp of El Viboro. He has held me captive for two weeks. You were my chance to escape. His men are drunk all the time, but he never drank. He watched everything, and had me tied every night.

We asked her name and she told us she was Anna Diaz and that the bandits had carried her away to be their servant. She told us, "I washed the shirt you took for the child to wear. A shirt of El Viboro. I was in the adobe when you were there with El Viboro. I was hiding in a corner behind the blankets hung on the rope. As soon as you went out the window, I followed. Thanks to God you had to travel slow, because my eyesight is so bad I cannot travel fast or find my way. I camped close by you last night, and I could smell the river. That is where I went this morning, only to find it flooding. I was hiding there in the cane when the last of El Viboro's men rode up. They are searching for you. I heard them say that they would return to their camp. They have much whiskey remaining. They will be there for at least another day. They think you killed the two bastards who led them. I saw the whole happening. The girl held the gun, but God fired it. I saw the entire thing. I hope they will fight to see who leads them now, and they all shoot themselves to the last one of the bastards."

All of us listened to her story. Even Consuelo seemed to comprehend what she was saying. She told us that she lived in La Mula,

Mexico, but had been only one week visiting her sister, Teresa Natividad, when she was carried away.

We both knew the Natividad families. One family lived close to Tornillo Creek on the north side of the Rio, and more lived on the south side. We questioned her and discovered she had been staying with the widow of Aurelio Natividad. His casa was five miles from the river, and it was on the side of the Rio that we were on.

Knowing the way to San Vicente could be flooded for days, and that the bandits would be searching for us, we decided to make our way to the house of Anna's sister. A slow and difficult way if we stayed away from the trails which the bandits would use. Considering Consuelo's wound, we estimated it would take us until late tomorrow if we began soon, and if Consuelo rode the burro where the terrain allowed.

First, we needed to drink as much water as we could hold, and that meant we had to return to the river and chance the bandits not sneaking up on us with no way to escape.

We looked up the trail and stood quietly

to hear any sounds of horses, then we went as rapidly as possible to the river. Our burro followed us. The drying mud on his legs began to crack, and pieces fell onto the ground as we hurried along.

We quickly dug a shallow depression just above the water's edge and placed a dam of rocks and mud and plant debris on the low side. Then we splashed the river's turbid water into the newly created reservoir until it was full. We then washed our faces by the edge of the swift flowing water. Consuelo splashed her hair and face while Anna Diaz held her injured foot above the water.

Anna said she had brought a knife, so we knew that we could cut into barrel cactus for water and carve into the hearts of sotol plants for something to eat before camping for the night.

When the grit and mud suspended in the water had mostly settled to the bottom of our reservoir, we took turns drinking all the water our stomachs could hold. Juan washed the mud from our burro and gently talked to him, while Anna rebandaged Consuelo's foot with a piece of dry cloth from the small bundle she carried. Then we set out for Casa Natividad, staying off trails horsemen would use, crossing canyons and bare ridges, and skirting hills.

CHAPTER 13

The way was steep in many places, and many times Consuelo had to be helped off the burro. The walking and climbing only allowed the gash to partly close and begin to heal, and fresh blood flowed out onto the bandage for us to see. She was very brave. Her wound was on her left foot; above the arch and below the ankle bone. We asked her, but she said she was not in great pain. She never complained, but we came to support more and more of her weight as we proceeded. Finally, through steep terrain where she could not ride, we took turns carrying her on our backs with her small arms wrapped around our shoulders.

Anna Diaz had been greatly mistreated by the bandits. She had bruises on her face and arms. We figured, she had at least fifty years, and her eyesight was not good at all. She said that she could see close, but not far. She laughed when she told us that she only could see what she was in, but not what she was going to be in, but she assured us that she would know the canyon which led from the river to her sister's house, once we came to it. We continued moving across the washes and ravines which led to the river, and where the way was vertical walls or too difficult to traverse, we would go to our right, away from the Rio, up the dry arroyos, searching for a way over to the next canyon.

Anna followed along behind us, and she was no trouble. She was thankful; telling us over and over again how God would bless us for being so kind. We told her the tale of what had occurred when we found Consuelo, and she assured us that we were correct in believing that Consuelo was sent by the Holy Virgin.

We halted our march while there was sufficient light to find a cactus for water and dig some sotol or lechuguilla for food. We were lucky and found a big rattlesnake. Pablo collected prickley pear pads and singed away the thorns in our fire when it was flaming at its highest. We fed them to our hungry burro. We ate roasted sotol heads and lechuguilla hearts and snake.

After sustaining ourselves, we made camp in a spot sheltered from the wind. Juan and Anna gathered a mound of straw for our bed and cover. Before it was completely dark, while the western sky was still a golden blue, four souls climbed under the straw and lay huddled together with the women in the middle. Juan slept by Consuelo. Every time Pablo awoke that night, he saw him awake, lying close against her, and once he was stroking her head like a father would do to soothe his child.

The sun found us a distance from where we had slept, and saw us cutting the top off a barrel cactus. Anna found a stick and poked the interior until we could scoop up handfuls of watery mush, put it into our mouths, and suck out the water and spit out the fibers. The day would be cool, and thirst would not be a big problem. Juan and Pablo led the way, with Consuelo on the burro, followed by Anna.

Before we had gone far, the burro, to make it over a low ledge of rocks, jumped unexpectedly, and Consuelo fell off backwards. Her head struck a large rock sticking out of the ground. We sat her up and found blood oozing from the back of her head. Pablo parted her hair at the wound and inspected it. It was an open cut to the skull, and he could not tell if her head was busted or not. Her blood was so thick from lack of sufficient water, that the wound clotted quickly, and we were thankful that she would not lose more blood than her foot had already cost her. She got to her feet by herself, said she was ready to continue, and asked us to help her onto the burro. We did, and we continued along with one of us on each side of the animal; ready to catch her if it should happen again. She tightly clutched the little animal's mane, and we walked along in silence.

It was afternoon when we had worked our way down into a low area thick with agave. Some of them had bloomed that summer and many stalks stood as high as telegraph poles.

"This is the way," said Anna. "My sister's adobe is up this way." She pointed up the canyon. "We go about two miles, then go left into a narrow, side canyon, then it is a short walk to where it widens. There will be water and cottonwood trees and my sister."

First we opened another barrel cactus, and Anna found a plant she could use to make a poultice for Consuelo's foot. Soon we were walking again, and we could see that the canyon had been used often as a cow path to the Rio Grande. Anna knew the way, and she walked ahead of us along the trail. Old manure and hoofprints told Juan and Pablo that a lot of horses had used this trail no more than 12 or so days before.

We came to a slit in tall, black, vertical rock face. Anna was telling us it was the entrance to the side canyon when we heard a distant gun shot echoing out of it. Then, we heard a woman's voice speaking, just loud enough for us to hear from where she sat on the hill above us. It was Teresa Natividad. "Anna, do not go in. The bandits are back. Come this way. Up here, pronto," she beckoned to us.

We joined her after struggling up a steep slope of loose rubble between stair-like ledges of gray rock. Without pausing, except to hug her sister, Teresa led us another half mile to a camp she had made.

When we stopped she told us that she had lived outside since the bandits had taken Anna. She said the bandits had returned that noon, and that Aurelio's brother and his wife had been staying with her. She said they had watched the south trail, taking turns all of each day, looking out for the bandits, and, also, hoping they would see me returning, but the bandits rode in from the west, across the mountains, and it was only luck that she and her visitors were out with the goats when they rode in. She said that she sent them to Rancho de la Pared for help and she had waited and watched the trail up from the Rio, hoping to see Anna. When she saw us, she said a thousand prayers had been answered.

Finally, she looked at Consuelo and said, “You are the daughter of Jesus Alvarez. I thought you were dead.” Looking at us she said, “And you are the Luna twins. Can you tell me why this child wears so little to cover her modesty? Where are the rest of her clothes?”

Pablo replied, “She wears a shirt we grabbed in our escape. It was clean, and longer, but we have used pieces of it to bandage her foot."

Teresa hugged Anna and Consuelo, then looked coldly at Juan and Pablo. She then addressed Consuelo, "I have a dress for you. You are not a little girl anymore. It is not good to wear so little in front of these two men. Any men." She looked at us again, with her eyes saying we were somehow guilty of the situation.

Consuelo, standing, supporting herself against the burro, looked solemnly at Teresa Natividad. She did not seem to hear Teresa's words. She implored her, "Please take me to the bandits. The blessed Virgin has asked me to bring them a message from her."

Teresa looked at her sister, then at Consuelo. She said, "Child the bandits at my house are the men of El Viboro. They are very dangerous. Some are searching for them for the murder of many people. They would kill you and worse, child. It is a miracle that my sister survived. El Viboro's men must be out searching for you four. Put on this dress." She helped Consuelo into a dress she had gotten from a bag.

Juan and Pablo were about to tell Teresa

that the bandits would probably kill them all, but we hesitated. We were more superstitious than religious. Our father said there was probably no Virgin; it was a story the Spanish had made up. But, we had seen the ball of fire. Could it be possible that Consuelo Alvarez was under the protection of the Virgin of the Spanish? And, in the glowing dust we had heard no words from Heaven. Was it that the words could only have been heard by a chosen one? Possibly, she could walk into the midst of the bandits again and come out alive, and all the bandits would either follow her to the church, or, if she was an avenging angel, they could all die at her hand, again guided by God—or, maybe, by the spirits known to our dead father to make the impossible happen.

While Pablo wondered these things Juan spoke, "They may be the gang of El Viboro, but El Viboro is not with them. Consuelo Alvarez held the gun that blew him to Hell, and then his lieutenant, El Gallo. They are both dead in pieces. Your sister, my brother, and me saw it happen."

"Yes, I saw it too," said Anna. "It could be seen as two providential events caused by

God, possibly, but possibly it was just fate catching up with two evil men."

Pablo finally spoke and told Teresa Natividad about the events when we first found Consuelo. He said, "What if she could walk into the bandits, and they were compelled to listen to her message from the Virgin, and they went to confession and were no longer bandits?"

Juan quickly replied, "No. It would not be safe here. We must go to Rancho de la Pared. People will be there. If the bandits are to hear the message of the Virgin from the mouth of Consuelo, it should be where there are more of us, and with guns. If God means for them to hear the Virgin's words, then they will ride to Rancho de la Pared and listen to Consuelo Alvarez while they are outside the walls of the rancho."

All of us, except Consuelo, thought this was a good idea. Consuelo began to limp out of the camp. Pablo grabbed her. She pleaded to be turned loose.

We lifted Consuelo onto the burro, then all of us set out for Rancho de la Pared. It would mean another night in the mountains, and a long walk the following day.

That night the three women slept together. Teresa Natividad handed a blanket to us and pointed to the place we were expected to sleep. She did not seem to like us very much.

CHAPTER 14

Rancho de la Pared was in ruins in 1910–the only time we had ever been there. It had once been a big cattle ranch until the patron lost interest after three years of no rain. He had returned to Mexico City before we were born.

In 1915 the hacienda included a rock casa of five rooms, and three adobes and a bunk house and barn, all surrounded by a ten foot wall of logs and adobe, for it was built during the last years of Comanche raids. It was once like a fort, but we walked past abandoned adobes outside the wall, and through a place where the wall was laying on the ground. The old rancho had, in a more recent time, become a little village. Inside the surrounding wall the houses all still had roofs, and some had corrugated tin that was not all rusted.

Consuelo, on our burro, Teresa and Anna, and Juan and Pablo were looking at a deserted place when a man walked out of the big casa and greeted us. It was Boca Toro. When he was sure who we were, he motioned toward the casa, and his wife, Desea, came out and stood by him.

He motioned for us to come to him and said, "Come and sit by our campfire and drink with us. The well has gone dry, everybody has departed, and we do not have a fire."

Boca Toro and his wife were Indians who proudly claimed no Spanish blood. They said they were Kickapoo, mostly, with a Comanche chief somewhere in their ancestors. The Spanish they spoke was mixed with Indian words. Desea was not named correctly. Maybe her name was a joke because she was muy ugly. She smiled with a toothless mouth. She had a tooth or two sometimes, and maybe she had happy eyes, but they were always squinted shut. But she had friendly ways, so we imagined her to have happy eyes.

Boca was a great talker. He had a long, Indian name which stated that fact, but Boca was an easier word to say, so that became his name. They both had survived many hardships, for they were both very old and wrinkled with wrinkles on wrinkles. They had lived in campsites most of their lives.

We went over and greeted them. Teresa asked, "Did you see the brother of my husband and his wife? They should have arrived here yesterday."

Boca answered, "Yes. They came and left with some others this morning. They are returning with water and food and some guns. We have no water. And your husband's brother's wife, she joined three of her cousins. They thought it best to hide at a place in the mountains, then return when the bandits are gone and things are quiet."

Boca kept on talking about less and less. We were thirsty so we suggested that we go to find some cactus water, but Boca said that all the cactus around had been used. It was all hacked up and rotting with flies, he said.

Teresa turned to face the well. Some of the rock wall surrounding it was missing, but the bucket still hung from the windlass. She asked, "The well is completely dry?"

Boca answered, "I think there is a bit of water, but it is too shallow for the bucket to find it. A strong man could go down to the bottom and use a cup to fill the bucket. I might get down, but I know I could not climb up."

Teresa and Anna turned to face us. We said nothing, then Pablo asked how deep was the well.

Boca Toro answered, "Deeper than a ladder is tall. About over twenty feet. If a man could climb down the rope, I think we could pull him out. Maybe? The shaft is very small because it has been made to have rock walls. A fat man could get stuck. I know a man who climbed to the bottom and back up, with no help."

Juan looked at Consuelo's parched, peeling lips and said, "I will go down," and he walked to the well and peered down into blackness. He noted the well shaft was three feet in diameter at its narrowest, so he decided he could get to the bottom and return.

Teresa also peered into the well. Then she began to spin the crank of the windlass, and the bucket went down out of sight into the darkness. We heard a sound when it hit bottom. We thought we heard a little splash.

"I will need a candle. I will need to

see," said Juan.

When he said that, Desea scurried into the great casa and soon returned with a candle lantern, a tobacco can, and a small flat stone. Boca took a wad of rubbed grass from his pocket and kneeled down by the lantern. He placed the grass ball on the flat stone, opened the tobacco tin, and poured a tiny bit of black powder onto the grass. Desea handed him two flint stones and he struck them above the powder. The powder flashed and caught the grass on fire. Desea took sticks from the bag she carried and placed them on the burning grass. Boca lit the candle, lowered the glass cover, then handed the lantern to Juan.

Juan stood with the lantern and looked down the well. He turned to them and said, "I cannot hold the candle and climb down the rope, and I do not want to climb down the well if I cannot see what is there."

Boca said, "The bottom is there. It will be there in the dark or by the light of the candle."

Teresa said, "Give me the lantern. When you get to the bottom, tell us and we will raise the bucket and send the light down in it."

Juan was not wanting to do it that way, but he realized it was the only way. Consuelo was thirsty and so was he. He grabbed the rope, tugged on it, then began to lower himself down the well.

Teresa sent the light down, along with a cup to scoop water. He yelled to them, "There is very little water. But, the side of the well at the bottom has been dug out for eight feet, and I can see water seeping out of the wall at the end. I need a pick to dig with. I think digging might bring more water."

Again, Desea went into the great house, and she returned with a pickaxe with a short little handle. Teresa lowered it down, and, soon, heard Juan digging.

Then all of those of us outside the well heard a wild yell and a gunshot from just beyond the wall.

Boca Toro shouted, "It is bandits. Everybody into the casa."

Pablo grabbed Consuelo before she could walk toward the bandits to deliver her message of salvation, and carried her over his shoulder. All of them, including the burro, rushed into the great casa, and Desea slammed the door behind.

Nine horsemen rode into the yard. Pablo looked out the cracks of a wood-barred window and saw some of the men he had seen at the camp of El Viboro. Two carried rifles and the others held pistols.

One shouted, “We just want some water and food. Boca Toro, who is in there with you? Come out. Let's talk. Do you have any guns?”

Pablo had been in holes in the ground and in mines, and he knew for a fact that if something is making noise, or there is talking, and it is not being done close above the hole, then very little, if anything, is heard in the hole.

Juan had heard nothing; not even the gunshot. He was still digging and talking to people who were no longer looking down into the well.

Pablo asked Boca, “Do you have a gun?” Boca went to the kitchen and brought back a bolt-action rifle. Pablo opened the bolt to find it empty and asked where the bullets were. Desea went to the kitchen, returned with a handful of bullets, and dumped them into his hand. They had all been taken apart. The heads had been pried from the shell and the powder had been emptied out.

Pablo asked, "Where in the name of God is the powder?"

Desea held up the tobacco tin.

"We have been using the powder to start our fires," said Boca.

Teresa excitedly asked, "Can we put the powder back into the bullets, then put them together to make a bullet again?"

Anna said, "Yes, I have done it before. But, I do not know how much powder. That is very important. My husband knew how much powder, but I can push the head into the shell."

They heard the bandit again ask if they had any guns. "Come on out," he repeated, "We just need a meal and a drink. Boca, you know me. I have never caused you or Desea any harm."

They had eleven bullets and thought they would divide the powder into eleven piles, but fearing the bandits were preparing to enter the house, Boca hurriedly put some powder into a shell, and Anna tapped the bullet head onto it. Pablo took the assembled bullet and placed it in the chamber and closed the bolt. He carried the gun to the window which looked out on the bandits.

The smallest bandit had dismounted, and he was standing between the well and the door into the great casa. While they were gathered around the window, trying to see through the boards, they did not see Consuelo leave and go onto the porch. They did not know she was outside until the standing bandit spoke to her, and they heard Consuelo reply, "I am Consuelo Alvarez. The Holy Virgin has told me to deliver her words to you."

Teresa and Anna ran to the open door to stop her, but Consuelo had stepped off the porch and was walking toward the bandit. Boca Toro grabbed them back and told them to stay inside.

Pablo watched as Consuelo arrived in front of the bandit, who grabbed her and held her in front of him. He waved his pistol around and said, "Now you will all come out. You do not want this pretty girl with a hole in her arm, do you? Or, maybe, her leg?"

Boca said that Consuelo would either be

killed, or the bandits would ride away with her, but we would never get her back. Then, fearing for the safety of Consuelo Alvarez, Pablo quit thinking about what to do. He pointed the rifle out the window, aimed high on the bandit's head, and pulled the trigger.

The sound of the gun was more of a poof than a gunshot, and Pablo could see the bullet traveling toward his target like it was moving a little slow for a bullet, but faster than an arrow. It hit the bandit in the center of his forehead and stuck there, half into his skull and half sticking out, and there was no blood. The bandit's pistol discharged into the dust, he staggered backward, still holding Consuelo, and both flipped into the well and disappeared from view.

At the bottom, digging at the end of the side tunnel, Juan had heard nothing of the happenings above, and he did not know that Consuelo and the bandit were coming.

The folded bandit slid down the well with his head and shoulders bouncing tight against one side, and his boots dragging the other. With a smacking thud, the bandit landed with Consuelo on top of him. The bandit was dead with a broken neck, but Consuelo was alive and unhurt, except for several growing knots on her head where it had bumped against the rocks on her trip down.

Juan held up the lantern and saw Consuelo trying to standup on the lifeless body of someone he did not recognize.

It was difficult for Juan or Pablo, and possibly anyone else, to know when Consuelo was acting normally or was dazed or ill. She always seemed to be floating along in her own world, except when she saw a bandit and would begin her speech.

Juan stared at the sight, then crawled to Consuelo and pulled her into the tunnel. He held the lantern above the man's head. He saw the bullet sticking out and discovered that the man was dead. He asked Consuelo what was happening. She replied that the man was a bandit and she had gone to him to deliver the message from the Virgin.

Juan, already knowing the outcome of her message in the presence of the bandits who had killed her family, knew that somehow Consuelo had gotten this bandit into the well.

He first thought she had lured him, shot him, then pushed him in. No, he said to himself, the girl was surely innocent— it would take a strong man to do those things. Still, he wondered with a dull suspicion fueled by lust pouring over guilt. Was this new and improbable event the action of a cunning, vengeful Consuelo, or divine intervention? He looked into her eyes and told himself that the Devil surely had the power to appear innocent. That light above Juniper Canyon had gone into the earth. It had not ascended to Heaven.

Then, he questioned her, "Did anyone put a crucifix in your hands? Who shot the bandit?"

"He is shot?" she said, seeming to be ignorant of that fact. "He was holding me, we were alone, then we went backwards and now here I am. Where am I?"

"You fell down the well." He watched Consuelo rub the back of her head. He watched as each upward stroke of her hand raised her long hair, revealing, then hiding, the cream-in-coffee complexion of her neck and shoulder. The enchantment ended when he wondered where were the others.

He yelled up the well, “Is anybody up there?” No answer. Nobody heard him.

The bandits had ridden out and dismounted behind the cover of the wall. Boca and all were inside the great casa. Occasionally a bandit would come out from behind the wall and fire a pistol. Nobody could safely get to the well, and nobody knew if anyone remained alive in it.

CHAPTER 15

The Cactus Man had awakened again. He had been asleep for a few hours after he had completed the story of Consuelo Alvarez and Juan Pablo. I had helped him out of bed and into his chair. He had sat without speaking—just staring down at the glass over the beans. A moment later, he lifted the glass, up righted it, and set it down. He moved the beans around, then separated out two of them. He looked at the two beans, then pushed them close for me to see.

Then he said, “These two are my Boca and Desea beans.”

Sure enough, I saw an Indian in profile, and, on the second bean, a face with only a nose among wrinkles.

Cactus Man went back to bed, and I continued writing from my notes taken during his earlier narration:

I did not know my life was to be so much changed when we first found Consuelo

Alvarez. That place is still there, of course, but it has never had another ball of fire. When I travel there and stand in the exact place in the Chisos, on the ledge where she stood, I see her like a ghost beside that tree. It is like we moved away, and all that remained was the stuff the trees and earth are made of. The geologist we once met was not correct when he said that the land will be the same when men no longer walk upon it. The place has changed. Parts of the sides of Juniper Canyon have fallen into the creek, and floods have carried the dirt away. Big rocks have rolled down. Great rocks I could not carry back to where they had rested. The way is different each year I visit there, except the way from the creek to the ledge. I keep that the same. There, I move the smaller rocks that roll down back up to where they were in 1915. One, about my weight, I can no longer return to its place. It seems determined to be in the creek. And the tree is old now, and its needles are barely green.

When you travel alone in a vast country you talk to yourself. For a time the one speaking is also listening, then, without companions, the one listening, or the one talking, becomes another person. That man then has two souls, and he can have very interesting conversations. I had a twin to talk with. It sounds good, but we became three souls. Two talked and the third came only to listen, and I think that we were both that third soul during those times.

Cactus Man's words had trailed off. He stared at the beans for a minute, then he said, "But, my mind wanders. Let me continue the story."

They were trapped in the great casa. It was that all were thirsty, and they could not make Boca Toro understand they did not want him to keep telling stories of how thirsty he had been in the past. He had just come to the end of a thirst story when he went into another room. They heard a creaking noise, then he returned with a dusty, gallon jug of clear glass of the kind some people put kerosene into.

He set it on the kitchen table and said, "If anybody feels they are as thirsty as I was in my last story, then, let us all share this water."

Anna replied, "In that last story you

were so thirsty you could not spit. My tongue is sticking to my mouth, so these may be the last words I can speak clearly."

Teresa informed her that she was already speaking as if her tongue was covered with glue.

All turned their heads and looked at Desea. She shrugged her shoulders to indicate that she had nothing to say, or possibly that she did not know how thirsty she was. Pablo noticed that her mouth had withdrawn into a wrinkle, and her red face only had a nose.

The strong Teresa spoke, "I am as thirsty as you were in the story about the time your horse ran away and you had to walk ten miles without water in July. Is that thirsty enough to pull the cork on that jug?"

Boca answered by pulling that cork and pouring a cup of water. He commented, "We each must only drink half a cup." And they did. It was one of those times that the water did not make it to Pablo's stomach, but sunk into the dry walls of his throat.

The bandits were still firing at the great casa every fifteen minutes. Teresa and Boca made another bullet.

Boca said, "Try this one. It has more powder." Pablo placed it into the rifle.

They stood by the window and watched the well and the bandits. The casa was secure. The heavy back and front doors were locked, as was the thick wood shutters on the windows. The bandits began to run out into view, two or three at a time, then dart back behind the wall. Boca said the bandits wanted them to shoot back, to find out if we had more bullets and make them waste bullets on wild shots.

"If you do not shoot they might come in closer and we could kill another one of them," Boca said, then added, "I think those idiots have water. Look how fast they move."

Pablo waited, ready with the rifle. After thirty minutes, Teresa handed him four more completed bullets.

In the bottom of the well, Juan had heard Consuelo speak about something other than her mission. She had told Juan that there were more bandits and that our people were in the great casa.

Juan looked up the well. He said, "I can hear nothing." He waited, then looked down and said, “I smell food. Do you smell it?”

Consuelo agreed, and the two began to search for the source. Consuelo leaned toward the deadman's shirt. “The odor is coming from under his shirt,” she said.

Juan felt around, raised the shirttail, and lifted out a cloth wrapped package. It held a few stale, rolled, corn tortillas holding some kind of filling. The tortillas were spotted with gray mold, but didn't smell too bad to eat, and they were very hungry. The digging had increased the flow of water enough for them to fill the cup, so they drank and ate while sitting at the back of the tunnel, away from the body, and in the light of the candle lantern.

Soon, after eating, Juan Pablo began to feel strange. At first Juan thought it was the air going bad. Juan had worked in mines where people would get sleepy and gasp for air, but he was not gasping. The air was good, he decided. Then, he began to see gold nuggets glistening in the sides of the tunnel, and the rivulet of water became a silver rope covered with jewels.

Juan had eaten one tortilla, and had given Consuelo the other two, which she had eaten hurriedly. They were facing each other, squatting, trying to keep their clothing off the wet floor of the tunnel.

Consuelo stared at Juan's face, then she moved her head to the side and looked beyond him, and began to smile. “She is coming,” she said, exhaling the words in an excited, breathy voice.

He turned and looked at the back of the tunnel and saw nothing, except the marks where his pick had split the rock. He moved so her view would not be blocked, and he decided to sit on the dead man. He had been on his knees or squatting for two hours, and he was fatigued. He asked the body to forgive him and heard the words, “De nada,” come from within his head and silently flow from his ears. He held the lantern above the face of the corpse and saw a black centipede mustache waving its legs beneath the two caves where it dwelled. He watched the undulating legs on the unmoving body until he heard Consuelo speak again.

“See the bright light? Look, it is her, the Blessed Virgin.”

Juan held the lantern higher, but he

could see nothing but the rich vein of liquid silver his pick had released to flow from the rock.

"When she begins to speak the light becomes ever brighter. See it?" She turned her head and looked at Juan.

He saw tears streaming down to her chin and saw her face exquisite with rapture, but he could see no light heralding the coming of the Blessed Virgin. He thought about why he could not see the light that brought tears to the eyes of Consuelo. Was it for the reason that he was not a Catholic? That he was not even a Christian? That he lusted for Consuelo's body?

Tears came into his eyes as he realized he was a heathen who believed in spirits; a heathen with sexual craving for the woman who was chosen to see and hear the Blessed Virgin. A sight that was denied him for what he was—a nasty, filthy animal with no god. He closed his eyes to keep from seeing Consuelo, but in his mind he saw the times on the journey from the camp of El Viboro to the hiding place of Teresa Natividad when Consuelo, half naked, had asked for him to boost her up a ledge, and he had stood beneath her pushing on her naked butt and bare legs. He saw the many times she looked down at him and smiled when his hands were on her flesh. He could not escape those now lurid thoughts, with eyes shut or open.

Then he felt his thoughts and vision leave his head and begin to float above him. He could see in all directions with no eyes, and he could see precious metals and jewels and Consuelo, but his body was nowhere to be seen or felt.

Consuelo sat with her legs folded under her and her knees together. Juan's consciousness floated near her, and it saw her back straighten as she bowed her head.

She then answered the light he could not yet see, "Yes, Mother, I have told them at each opportunity. They do not seem to hear your words."

Juan heard only Consuelo, and he tried to cease thinking of his desire for her body as she continued speaking.

"Oh, blessed Mother, I understand. But I am already at the spring. You have sent me here. Yes, he is that man and he sits behind me. He dug into the rock where you stand. He brought forth the waters that flow beneath you. I will tell him that it is God's will through the Mother of Christ, and that now is the time."

Consuelo looked at Juan and held out her hand for him to join her. Somehow, he had returned to his body and now sat beside her. Consuelo held his hand between hers.

"I will Holy Mother. She says for you to place your other hand on mine." He did.

"Yes," said Consuelo.

Juan heard her repeat the word five times, then she turned to him and said that he must say, yes. He did. Then he admitted that he could not hear the Virgin, or see anything holy. Consuelo said, "I will tell you that you are blessed and forgiven, and that we are married by the Blessed Virgin in the name of God. She has instructed me to lie with my husband and conceive a child, and the child will help save the souls of the bandits."

Juan, alternately entering and exiting his body, became filled with fear. He shouted at her, "I understand now. You are not an angel. You are crazy and seeing things which are not there. We are in the bottom of Hell. We may die here. Consuelo, listen to me. We must try to climb out of here, now. Before the fires come."

"No," replied Consuelo, "the Virgin says we must conceive at this moment. You must lay with me now."

With those words, Juan began to forget about being in Hell. The power of the Virgin entered into him, and he cared not if she was only a mythical Spanish Virgin. He saw the Virgin's presence emerge and grow ever brighter and stronger when Consuelo raised her dress and was naked in the light of the candle lantern. "Devil or Angel," he thought, "This is just a dream. We are not here."

It was a dead man's body he braced his feet against as he energetically screwed Consuelo Alvarez and began to dream that he was doing work ordained by the Virgin of God's creation, then all his consciousness, as a shower of sparkles, ejected into the squirming evangelist.

He heard Consuelo tell someone, "You are such a good husband," then she shivered and shouted God's name and blessed the Holy Virgin.

CHAPTER 16

I had just worked up to the place in Cactus Man's tale where Juan had sex with his new bride, when Cactus Man had come awake and had sat up.

Standing by his bed, he said, “My body is telling me it is through with all that coffee. I have to go outside.”

When he had returned, he sat down at the table. I told him I was working on his story; making it understandable to people who would read it. I said I was at the place where Juan and Consuelo were in the well at Rancho de la Pared.

Cactus Man then said that he was at Rancho de la Pared just before Christmas. There was no well there. The place was abandoned and the metal roofs were gone, and the hacienda had no wood parts. It had all been carried away or burned in campfires.

He had continued speaking, When we were young, it was that many people lived in the Big Bend. Once the grassland was eaten and the trees cut, rains washed the soil away, and people no longer could have gardens. It may be difficult for you to believe, but in my lifetime this was a place of fertile valleys and terraces where gardens grew with corn and beans and squashes and melons. People were happy and prosperous, and the families had many children. By nineteen twenty they began to be starved out and entire families would suddenly be gone; leaving their adobes and furniture and walking away with what they could carry to Ojinaga and Presidio, and north to cities on the east-west highways. The people who stayed are mostly miserable, and they have forgotten the old ways. But, they stay here, clinging to life along the Rio Grande.

After the Catholic church closed, my father's hat came to me in a dream. It tumbled along in the wind. I followed it into the church the priests had abandoned, and it landed on a statue of a saint. I watched as the hat lowered itself, eating the statue until the hat set on the pedestal and the statue was devoured. The hat burped so loudly that it shook the church and plaster fell from the ceiling. It then flew out the doors and sailed into the mountains. Now, when I am with the spirit of my father, he wears no hat and his head is covered with dust. I think he dwells in a plant beside a dirt road where passing cars dust him often.

He quit speaking. I wrote a few lines to catch up. Then, I looked up at him as he said, "I am tired again. I think I will lie down."

I told him that I was going to stay up and work on his story. He told me I was a good man, and he lay down and soon was asleep.

I continued reading my notes and writing:

Boca and Pablo kept a lookout at the window. The bandits were still jumping out from behind the wall, but they did not fire a pistol every time anymore. All in the casa feared for Juan and Consuelo in the well and wished for some way to help them—if they were alive.

Boca Toro began to tell stories about times when he had been very hungry. Teresa and Anna listened to him while Desea slept in a chair. He was telling about a time when his belly button touched his backbone before he could find a meal. He said he was near death when a skunk came close to him. He grabbed the skunk and skinned it and ate it raw. He said, except for the odor, it tasted like goat.

Before he could begin another starvation story, Teresa said to him, "Do we have to hear another wild fable before you tell us there is something to eat that you have been hoarding?"

Boca said nothing, went into another room, and after the creaking board sound, returned with a bag of masa flour. Desea jumped up from her chair and grabbed the bag and carried it to the kitchen. She built a fire on the kitchen floor and mixed water into the masa. Soon all were eating tortillas.

Teresa asked, "Do you have any stories about how long you went without butter or syrup to eat with your tortilla?" Boca said, no, then a mouth appeared below Desea's nose and she laughed and laughed.

It was close to sundown when Boca said to Pablo, "You must shoot at them once before it is dark. We want them to know you have more bullets before we cannot see them. They will stay away if they think you can shoot them."

Pablo had seen Boca Toro many times at Boquillas del Carmen. Boca had never seemed too smart. He just knew him as a talker. Always talking about stupid things, and talking and talking from sober to drunk, and back to sober. But now Pablo saw a man who was suddenly smart. He knew Boca had a good idea. They needed to show the bandits that they had bullets so they would not sneak to the windows in the night.

Boca said, "They are cowards. They only had nerve behind El Viboro. They are coyotes, not wolves."

Pablo pointed the rifle at the place they would run to when they jumped from behind their wall. He aimed and waited with the gun barrel not showing outside the window.

Soon three of them jumped into view. The one in front quickly raised a whiskey bottle and swigged some. When he turned to hand it to the man behind him, Pablo fired. The rifle exploded and kicked his shoulder hard. Pablo fell back on his ass, and pieces of the rifle hit the ceiling. Boca had put more powder into that bullet—much more powder.

Boca helped him up and they looked out at the bandits. The superior bullet had killed the front two men, passing through them, and the third was slowly crawling back to the wall with a part of the bullet in his chest. He stopped crawling and lay still.

With the man who was probably their new leader in the well, and three more of them on the ground, the remaining bandits, coyotes that they were, did not like the odds. They galloped away taking four riderless horses with them.

They knew the bandits would not soon return. All ran to the well and discovered that Consuelo and Juan were alive, but somehow sounded crazy. Juan tied the bucket rope around Consuelo's waist and she was lifted out. They then pulled out the body of the bandit. Juan filled the bucket with the fresh water coming from the tunnel, put the bandit's pistol in his shirt, and then he climbed up the stone wall.

We hauled the four bodies downwind, and laid them out just over a rise. Consuelo and Anna thought the bodies should be buried.

We told them to do it. They stood by the scene, crossed themselves, and soon returned to us. They were not able to bury the bodies.

We all sat outside until it was night. We listened to Boca who talked and talked until Desea went into the great casa and lit some candles. We followed her and saw her when she reached into a closet behind a remnant of curtain and brought forth a bow and some arrows.

Boca said, "Desea goes to hunt a rabbit. I will build up the fire."

Desea turned to face us. We were surprised. It was the first time any of us had seen her face in dim light. Her squinting eyes, which in daylight were just bigger wrinkles, now were as large as an owl's. She faced us, then went out the door. Boca told us that she always returns with a rabbit or two. And she did.

That night we all slept well after sharing two rabbits, tortillas, and clear, well water. Juan and Consuelo said nothing about their marriage dream, and they both had recovered from their ordeal—at least they had ceased to utter queer statements about other people in the well with them. Teresa, Anna, and Consuelo spent the night together. Boca and Desea snored in the kitchen, and we brothers shared a blanket.

CHAPTER 17

We waited at the desolate rancho for two days after the bandits rode away. Nobody returned. Cold weather blew in from the north on that second day. The wind was strong and sand and dust swirled around in the plant-less courtyard inside the walls. It blew away the buzzards circling over the bodies we had dropped as far from the hacienda as we could carry them.

The winds traveled on south and the air became still. The new, freezing temperature changed the distant, hazy purple mountains to a cold, icy blue, and our breath became visible. We searched for firewood but returned only with armfuls of dead, dry, cactus pads and greasewood stems which, even though were green, would burn if set upon kindling. We dared not burn the boards over the windows, because they offered protection from bandits. We spent a first part of that night trembling and freezing until Teresa said we should all sleep in one bunch. Everybody then joined Boca and Desea in the kitchen floor. We pressed tight against each other with our few blankets spread to cover us all.

In the morning we found a sheet of ice on top our water. We were miserable and hungry, and down to eating seared lechuguilla tubers when we decided it was time to depart Rancho de la Pared. We figured that nobody was coming from Boquillas. We did not know if Aurelio's brother and the other few who had departed had ever made it to Boquillas, and if they had, would they be able to talk some men with guns into leaving to ride out of town when outlaws were in the vicinity.

So we departed with Consuelo on our burro. We had the pistol and its holster and belt of bullets taken from the bandit who had fallen into the well, and we carried a bucket and cup, and Boca's thirst-story jug, all full of water. Where the road sloped down to weave among hillocks of gravel, we paused and turned to see the last view of the walled hacienda, then headed down the road to Boquillas. Boca had cut all the blankets so we could each wear one like a poncho. He had given Consuelo two and she wore both. Her foot had healed enough to no longer bleed if she did not misuse it. Teresa and us led the way, Anna walked beside the burro and said she was prepared to catch Consuelo should she fall off. Boca, wearing a black, western hat with three, long, buzzard feathers rising above the band, walked in front of Desea who carried her bow and a quiver holding two rabbit arrows and five war arrows. She was wearing three necklaces with silver spoons obviously cut away from their handles, and a braided, horsehair belt with pieces of polished stone set into folded, hammered tin can lids which were sewn to the belt. We walked toward the morning sun, and, all squinting our eyes, appeared to be from the same parents—Boca and Desea.

It was when the sun was above our right shoulders that we heard the first distant gunshots. We halted and stood quiet, trying to hear.

I must tell you that gunfights were not like in the movies where all fired many bullets. Bullets were hard to come by, and you would try to not waste any and run dry. Then, you were dead if the enemy had even one remaining, and they knew your gun was dry.

We strained to hear how often the guns sounded. In about five minutes we heard eight shots, and that told us it was a big fight among many guns.

Boca said, "I think it is the rescue party fighting with bandits. That is where they have been."

Believing him, we all stared at Consuelo Alvarez. Anna grabbed Consuelo's leg and came to the front of the burro. We all expected Consuelo to begin pleading to be allowed to ride to the bandits, but, instead, she said, "We should go help them."

Us brothers looked at each other. We both wondered the same thing, and so did Teresa, who then asked Consuelo, "Help who? Help the bandits to discover the evil of their ways? Send you to them to tell them of your vision? Or help fight the bandits?"

Consuelo replied, "I will call to the bandits. We have the pistol. It will keep them away from us. They will have to listen to the message I carry."

Boca stepped forward. He had proved

himself wise at the rancho, and we were all ready to hear his advice. “We have the pistol. If we go and see the situation; see if it is possible to get the bandits into a crossfire, if that is possible, then we would see them ride away. Remember, they are mostly coyotes. They enjoy an advantage, but run when things get tight.”

All agreed that we would carefully go and look the situation over. It sounded like the shooting was at least a mile away. Boca said that the road ahead swung to the left before dropping into a canyon. He said that it sounded like someone had been ambushed in the canyon, and that was a good place to shoot down from ledges onto people on the road below.

Boca and Desea led us away from the road and into the greasewood sparsely covering an expanse of mounds of gray and yellowish volcanic ash sprinkled with head-sized, dark brown chunks of basalt. Boca said the way would lead us to the top end of the canyon where the road entered it. There we could see what was happening.

The mounds got higher and steeper, and

the footing was loose when Consuelo slid over the rump of the burro, and tumbled onto the ground. Naturally, her butt hit the loose clay, and her head fell back onto a chunk of hard basalt. She was knocked-out. We rushed to her and set her up.

After a moment she came to consciousness, looked back at the rock, and said, "I never fell from a burro before I saw the Lady. Why is this happening?"

Anna answered, "God tests those sent to do His work. You are having trials and tribulations like in the Bible. He is testing you from head to foot."

"I will pray for Him to not test my head anymore, and test another part of me that is not sore and so covered with bumps."

Teresa began to speak in her best severe voice, "Child, are you questioning God's . . ."

Our laughter interrupted her. All, even Consuelo, all but Teresa laughed at what Consuelo had just said. None ever had suspected that Consuelo was capable of being humorous.

"There is nothing funny about this," Teresa shouted above the laughing. "We are in danger. Others are in danger. Nothing is funny about this."

We brothers looked at each other and thought that maybe Teresa did not like Consuelo.

Consuelo began to reply, "What I meant was. . ."

Anna interrupted, "It is well, Consuelo. Perhaps we should not laugh so. You merely had a moment of lightheartedness. That is what it was. You have been through more than a heavy heart could continue to bear. I hope we can all live through this and all laugh again, someday."

All stood silent. Two more distant shots sounded. Boca grabbed the rope on our burro, and we all continued on foot.

Soon we were just one rise away from the sound of the gunfight. Boca said his eyes were not too good, and he asked us brothers to sneak up and see what the situation was.

At the top of a small ridge of gravel we were ten feet above the road. We peeked over the ridge at the ruins of an adobe that set on our side of the road just where the road began to drop down into the canyon in a series of three narrow switchbacks. Above where the road below straightened, we saw men at the rim. They were taking turns shooting at someone in the bottom on the road. They had someone pinned down. Another man standing back from the rim wore a white shirt and we could see the bandoleras crossing his chest—the usual sign of bandits.

We returned to our group and told them. We said that it seemed possible that we could see who was being shot at if we could get to the ruin and see down the canyon.

Deciding to stick together, all of us then walked around to the right and found low ground and approached the ruin. Soon we were there. Consuelo, Teresa, and Anna squatted behind the first wall, and the men and Desea crawled to what remained of the wall facing the shooting.

There, in the canyon on the side of the road away from the bandits, we saw five men firing from behind the protection of boulders. They had horses, and that told us the reason the bandits were so determined. The action was at a distance from us that if you held your thumb as far from your eye as you could, the nail would easily hide a horse. The bandits were out of range for our pistol, even though it was a 44 with a long barrel.

We watched as the man who had been standing back from the rim dropped and crawled to the edge. He yelled some words we could not understand. But the canyon walls directed the words of reply to our ears, and we heard a voice from the bottom shout, "I do not believe you. You will take our horses and food, and still kill us. You murderous bastard."

"My God," exclaimed Teresa, "That is my husband's brother. He will be killed."

Desea watched as two of the bandits fired into the canyon, then she said something to Boca using all Indian words unfamiliar to the rest of us.

Boca then told us, "It is a standoff. The men on the rim want the horses of the men in the canyon. They are shooting above the horses, into the rocks behind the men on the canyon floor. Neither side can see the other. Nobody wants to get his head shot off. A death would be an accident. The men in the bottom maybe do not know this, but they could run to where we are and not be seen if they stayed close to the cliff under the bandits. But, then, the horses might be lost. Or something could go wrong—some bandits are more treacherous and do not play a fair standoff."

All of us then looked at the situation and agreed. Boca assured us again that all we had to do is fire the pistol at the would-be horse thieves several times to scare them away with the threat of a crossfire. Then he backed off a bit and said, "It has a good chance of working."

Teresa heard him say those words and asked as loudly as she dared, "What do we do if it does not?"

"It has a good chance," he replied. "The men and the horses down at the road will be saved if it does."

Teresa crawled forward and peered at the men in the canyon. She agreed that we must help them, but, when she said the words, the idea came to us brothers that Consuelo's presence would cause divine intervention to come to our aid and protect us, and kill a bandit or two.

All were ready for anything as Juan

checked the pistol. Then he stood up behind a taller piece of the adobe wall, to the left of the bottom half of what had been a window. All of us watched the distance, we heard the cocking of the hammer and held our breath. A bandit fired a rifle into the canyon, then all of the gang lay motionless, looking down toward their quarry. None of us glanced back at Consuelo Alvarez, who in that few, breathless, timeless parts of seconds, had moved forward, and pushed upward on Juan's outstretched gun arm, at the time he pulled the trigger.

The shot hid part of her first word and all we heard was, ". . .o! I must talk to them first."

Too late. All of us watched to see the bullet make dust, and then see the gang's reaction to the new situation. The bullet, because its path had been changed by Consuelo, rose upward toward the bandits, then fell into the middle of their line. It must have been a fresh bullet. People sometimes had old bullets they had carried for a long time, but that bullet was probably factory fresh and ready to go far.

We looked on, saw no sign where the

bullet had landed, and the bandits did not react. Then we saw them pointing in our direction, and all but one crawled back from the rim and ran low into a gully which faced the canyon.

Soon we saw them sticking their heads up and looking toward us. One of them still lay where he had been when we fired. His rifle still pointed forward. Two men rushed from the gully and carried the unmoving man and disappeared behind some boulders.

Juan fired a second time, dust jumped in front of the gully, and all the heads disappeared from our view. We looked down into the canyon and saw a man waving a sombrero at us. Then that man was fired upon from the gully by someone away from our view. Our plan did not appear to be working.

We did not know that the first bullet had killed the last living nephew of the leader of that gang, and that El Viboro had been the leader's last living son. They opened fire on us and used a dozen or more bullets. All of us kissed the ground as pieces of adobe flew in the air.

Boca Toro shouted, "Those bastards

usually would run now. They seem to be upset with us. They badly need the horses, or you killed somebody important." He raised up and looked, sat back and said, "I think some of them are getting to their horses." He raised up again and then reported, "Three of them are riding to the right. I bet they will cross that gully when they can, and come up in the rocks across the road from us. We will be in a crossfire."

But, Consuelo had already done something that would alter the coming calamity. She was across the road when we glimpsed her entering a field of huge boulders.

Desea took off after her. Then Juan and Pablo, now with the pistol, followed.

Realizing they had no weapons, the rest of them also ran from the adobe and followed into a labyrinth of boulders and ravines.

Consuelo's foot had suddenly recovered, and she became, once again, a fleet-footed zagala, and we were not gaining much on her.

Back about five hundred feet from the road, in an area of boulders and tall rock spires lining winding, shallow arroyos, we spotted her in front of us. We were running toward her when she went out of our view, over a crest.

We arrived at that place in time to see Consuelo lose her footing, cartwheel through the air from atop a rock, and pass just in front of the lead horse of the flanking group of three bandits. As she spun, her blanket poncho flared out, making her appear large and strange to the horse, which reared and fell back onto its left side. The panicked horse rose and began running with the rider's booted foot held tightly in the left stirrup. The other riders went forward to aid him, but his head had bashed into several large rocks, and he had already been dragged to his death.

Consuelo had seen none of it, and she was standing unhurt, dusting and adjusting her blankets, when the other two riders turned and rode toward her. They did not see Desea until she had shot a war arrow into the lead rider's side. He fell death-wounded from his horse as we fired a fresh bullet into the other rider. That wounded rider then swung his horse around, and, in a blind panic, he wildly emptied his six-shooter, once into his own leg and horse, while Desea shot a rabbit arrow into his neck at the same time as we again fired the pistol.

Three more bandits were well dead.

Boca, Teresa, and Anna did not know what was happening just over the rise they stood behind. They did not know who had won the battle of eight shots, or which way to run. They waited anxiously.

Then Consuelo appeared on top and saw them. She shouted, in a disappointed voice, “They are killed.” Between those words and the ones that quickly followed, they had all feared she meant us and Desea, because there had been so many gunshots.

Consuelo arrived crying and still talking, “Before I could tell them the words of the Holy Virgin, they were all on the ground, dead. I am a disgrace to our Lady.”

Desea loomed up to stand beside her. We climbed among the rocks toward each other and helped carry three rifles, three pistols and holster belts, and six bandoleras, each still with at least a third of their loops holding rifle bullets. The pistol belts and bandoleras were sticky with already drying blood.

All thought it best to return to the safety

of the four walls of the adobe. Boca asked about the horses and Desea answered that she had unsaddled them thinking that they would return to the bandits, who, with three extra horses, would decide to leave.

Within the ruin Desea revealed what she had found in a bandit's saddlebag—about four pounds of jerky. All of us ate and chewed until our jaws were sore.

There was no early night moon when Boca told us that we must quietly leave the ruin and sleep elsewhere to be safe from a sneak attack. We walked about thirty minutes into an area across the canyon from the bandits, and we spent the night there. Among all our hushed guesses about the next day, none of us suspected what was to happen.

CHAPTER 18

The Cactus Man had awakened again during the early hours after midnight. He went to the hutch and searched for some missing beans. He rummaged in a drawer and brought out a film can. Sitting down at the table he had commented, “Here they are. These are the last of the bandits that killed the family of Consuelo Alvarez.”

Cactus Man had then returned to his bed, and he was soon sleeping again, while I continued his story:

The night brought us two brothers to share what had passed at Rancho de la Pared when we were not together. We spoke of the events in the well and of a visions of gold and silver and gems, and a marriage to an angel in the glow of Heavenly light. We spoke of seeing a bullet in flight and told of the rifle which killed three men and itself with one shot.

We slept in dreams that night. In the morning of that night we were each other again, and we ate jerky with the others. It was before dawn when we set out to find a defensive position; hopefully one that could also help the brother of the husband of Teresa.

Our starving burro had departed in the night to search for food. Boca had said that the burro would do that, and we all thought it was best for the burro, especially before it was necessary to eat him. The people of the Big Bend would eat horse or dog before eating burro. It was a tradition among the starving. We had two pounds of jerky remaining, and a full jug of water.

Being north of the road where it ran along the bottom of the canyon, we made our way south between boulders and through narrow, rock-lined passages. Consuelo walked in the middle of our line so we could watch her and keep her corralled.

Desea, with good eyes, led the way back to the canyon's edge. She motioned for us to get down, then she crawled to a place where she could best see the other side and the men in the bottom. Returning to us she said that nobody was anywhere—no bandits, no horses alive or dead, no brother of the husband of

Teresa Natividad.

It was cold, the sun was just up, and, back away from the canyon's edge, we sat in the sun, warming ourselves and eating jerky. We made no conversation, but remained alert, listening for any sign of danger. Lizards began crawling out to bask. The only sound was our jawbones clicking as all of us chewed the tough jerky. Boca, in a hushed voice began a story about a starving time when he prayed for food and how that had resulted in a rain of tortillas. Teresa and Desea told him to shut up. He chewed without any further comments except to insist that he was sure it was burro jerky we ate.

The reason that the road was in the bottom of the canyon was that the country on either side was a jumble of huge boulders and rocks sticking up as high as fifteen feet. On either side of the canyon there were difficult zigzagging ways for horses to get through, with a few treacherous climbs over piles of round rocks, but there was no path wide enough for a wagon or cart.

We decided to return to a place where we could view the ruin, because Teresa, not exactly knowing why, had come to believe that the brother of Aurelio Natividad could be there. Desea scouted it and told us that five men were in the ruin, with three horses also within its walls.

Teresa climbed to the rise overlooking the road, recognized her brother-in-law's horse, and cried out, “Jose, are you there? It is Teresa with the people who were in the ruin yesterday.”

Jose answered and told us it was safe to come down, and that they had heard or seen no activity since yesterday's gunfight.

They had food and water, but not too much water. The day would be a comfortable temperature, not hot, not cold, and not much was needed.

One among them was a man from England. He was called Louis London, and he spoke what he called Castilian Spanish. All understood him, but his accent sounded funny to us. He had green eyes, white skin below his collar, and had around forty years in age. He was dressed like a vaquero, and he was not obsessed with bathing, like the stories of my grandfather who repeated tales of Castilian

Spaniards who once lived in northern Mexico and would often bathe in tubs of warmed water. Jose Natividad told us that he had met Louis in Boquillas del Carmen last spring, and that they had been friends since that time. Two Mexicans with them we knew from the mines and driving freight—cousins, Erasmo and Domingo Reyes, who both wore crossed bandoleras and carried Winchesters. The third man, he called himself only, Julio, had been seen around the local mining towns in Mexico for the last summer.

Louis told us that we were in a bad spot; too many high places around us from where we could be shot, and there was no safe way to retreat. He seemed knowledgeable of matters of gunfights. Boca asked him if he was a soldier, then he told us that he had been a sailor who had once fought on the sea, and that he was purposely as far from the sea as he could get.

All agreed that we should leave the ruin and head toward Boquillas, but not down the canyon. Julio, who had been slow to introduce himself, and seemed shy, said the easiest way back was across the road on the south side of the canyon. Boca said, “It would be safer to stay on the north side. I have traveled there before. I think I can remember a way through that is easy. But, you would have to walk your horses over some places.”

Consuelo, who had seemed more aware than usual of what was being discussed, asked us, “Where are the bandits now? How many remain?”

Jose answered her, “Last night in the dark we came to this ruin. Nobody was here. But, we heard horses just south of here during the night. This morning we heard nothing. There was a rumor in Boquillas, however, before we departed, that a big gang of bandits is riding north from the mountains and toward the Rio Grande. They are being chased out of the south country by soldiers. That is the rumor.”

There was nothing remaining to do but set out for Boquillas—two to three days on foot. So, all departed the ruin, and we made our way along the north rim of the canyon. There was twelve of us, now, with eight rifles and nine pistols. We felt better about the situation and hoped to make it to Boquillas without encountering any trouble. Desea and one of the cousins scouted ahead, and the rest followed several hundred feet behind. Julio, leading his horse, walked behind us all, and Boca kept turning to see where Julio was.

In two hours we were above the east entrance into the canyon passage. Desea came back to us and said that in the open country ahead, to the southeast, was the dust of many riders about two miles away.

We quickly hid ourselves in the rocks just below the top of a rise. From that spot we saw thirty bandits ride onto the road and enter the canyon at a gallop. Soon they were past.

Boca said, “Something tells me they are looking for us personally. Yesterday, and maybe at the rancho, someone important, maybe a relative, was killed. The man who dropped into the well appeared important. You think so? The leader's brother, maybe?”

Domingo Reyes said, “That bunch has trackers with them. I recognized two of them—their fathers were Apache. If they seek us, they will track us from the ruin, and be on us before the daylight is gone.”

Louis spoke up, “One of us must ride

for help. The rest must find a good place to fight from. I do not see any other choices. Anybody suggest another idea?"

Boca asked, "Whose horses are with us?"

Julio replied, "The pinto is mine. As you can see, he is in good condition. I can be in Boquillas this evening if I start riding now, and with a spare horse to start out on."

Boca, sounding suspicious, asked him, "Where are you from? Where does your family live?"

"My family farms on the Rio Conches– the Zamas family."

"Erasmo, do you know this man?"

"Si, Boca, he has been good company since last July."

Boca looked Julio up and down. He noticed the young man carried a new rifle and a new pistol. His dark blue clothing appeared not very worn. Even his two bandoleras were polished and showed little wear. He recalled seeing well-cut hair when Julio's sombrero had once been knocked from his head by an overhanging ledge. Boca thought about all that, and said, "We must decide who goes.

Whoever it is, they must travel with only a pistol and three bullets. Those remaining will need the rifles and ammunition."

Boca expected Julio to decline such an offer, or at least argue for his rifle and more bullets, but Julio readily agreed; too quickly for Boca to not know there was something going on. He spoke to Desea so only she could hear, then he asked all of us if it was a good idea to allow Julio to ride for help.

Louis answered, "I have seen the Reyes cousins shoot. They are good shots. We are better off having them with us. What if one of the women rode for help?"

Teresa and Anna agreed they did not wish to be parted, and added that they were not experienced enough to ride a running horse all day. Consuelo could not be trusted to find the way, and we knew that her sore head could not withstand a fall from a running horse. Also, what if a woman rode into bandits on the road? We all looked at Julio.

Julio chose from the two other horses—one of them belonging to Jose, and the other to Domingo. It seemed that two horses had somehow mysteriously disappeared during their night in the ruin. He picked Jose's roan gelding. Then he suggested that it would be less of a chance of not making it to Boquillas if he took two extra mounts. Boca told him we may need one to eat.

With none of the food or water, except a swig before riding out, Julio departed, riding toward the road on the roan, leading his pinto on a short length of rope. All of us but Desea waved adios.

We watched the man and horses appearing out of the last arroyo before the road, and then we saw the unthinkable as he spurred his mount and headed into the canyon.

"What the hell!" exclaimed loud voices in Spanish and English.

We all turned and stared at Boca, who was speaking loudly for all to hear, "It is probably that we are going to get those horses back. Watch and see who comes from the canyon."

In about fifteen minutes, out rode Desea, bareback on Jose's roan. We all watched while she appeared out of the arroyo beside the road, and worked her way back up to us.

Arriving with one less war arrow in her

quiver, she dismounted and told Boca, "You saw his game before me. I must be having too many years."

Boca walked to her and embraced his wife and said, "No. I saw your face out of the corner of my eyes while he spoke. You knew him at the same time I did."

Desea then told us all, "It went well. I jumped up from behind cover as he approached, and I shot him as he passed within ten feet of me. His horse slowed when startled by my sudden appearance. It was easy, just like I knew it would happen. He fell and the pinto tripped on the dragging rope. The roan returned and I set Julio's body against a rock facing up the canyon. I posed him to look like he is having a siesta. His sombrero is over his eyes. He looks good. His pinto is saddled and tied near him."

Louis said, "I wondered how anybody showing up in Boquillas could expect to find enough men and guns. Jose could only talk me and the other three into coming when there were rumors of so many banditos. How did you know Julio was a bandit?"

Boca replied, "He was hard to see. At

first I thought he was shy. I gave him a chance to show himself. Better to be without him in a fight, I thought, then to take the chance on him. Now when we signal the bandits, they will return and pause where Desea put the 'sleeping' Julio. Four of us will be on the ledge above them. We must go quick now."

Boca stated his plan and all agreed to it. It was Apache guerrilla warfare. Four of us, the best riflemen, carrying only Winchesters, would leave immediately and ambush the bandits from the canyon ledge above Julio's siesta. After two or three shots each, and hopefully the death of four to six bandits, the four would run back to a second position at our end of the canyon, at the place Boca expected the bandits to ride if they continued the battle. In three groups would be our army, hidden with guns ready. Boca and Desea would lie in wait to the bandit's left and hope to get a few clear shots after we open fire. We would all fire and withdraw out of sight of the bandits until we were in a last defensive position under an overhanging ledge where nobody could come up behind us, or have a shot from above.

The best rifles, one of us with Jose,

Louis, and Erasmo, led by Desea, headed for the canyon rim above where Julio sat. After ten minutes, Boca fired Julio's pistol once, waited a moment, and rapidly fired two times into the air from the mouth of the canyon.

While this occurred, the others carried the food, water, and blankets, and led the horses to the place where everybody was to meet, eventually, if all survived. There, Consuelo, watched by Anna, would remain during the skirmishes. We handed Anna a pistol and holster belt, which she put on.

Meanwhile, some members of the bandit gang had heard one or all the shots. Others who had been talking or sleeping had heard nothing. Their leader, known as El Casco, the father of El Viboro and uncle of El Gallo, was seeking the men who had killed them. A man went to him in the ruin and told him shots had been heard, then El Casco ordered all to mount, and they rode back into the canyon.

The bandit leader had another reason for finding them. In his thoughts was a fantasy, an intuition, that the girl who accompanied the killers of his sons, now carried his grandson. Three of the bandits who attacked at Rancho de la Pared had been in the gang of drunks when El Viboro died. They had told El Casco that El Viboro had screwed the girl who they had seen again at the rancho, and now, El Casco, with no sons remaining, was sustained by the belief that his family would live on if he could find that girl and keep her and the grandson alive—a grandson that his mind had driven him to be so sure she carried.

The band of outlaws arrived at a gallop and pulled up when they saw Julio. They did not have time to scan the canyon rims before four rifles opened up. The first bullets all hit targets and three men fell from the saddle. The second round of fire killed two more and wounded one. Only Jose and Erasmo each had a good third shot, and two more bandits were struck.

Bandits began firing up at the place where gun smoke drifted in the air, but we were gone from the canyon's rim.

It became that three groups of us lay in ambush above the road's exit from the canyon. Us brothers and Louis held the center, with Desea and Boca on our right and down closer to the road, and Teresa, Erasmo, and Domingo about a hundred feet to our left.

We did not know if the bandits would come. Everything was quiet. We kept looking behind us at our route to the next, higher place we were to fire from. Still, nobody came from the canyon.

First we saw the dust rising above the rim, then the gang rode into view and halted on the road. One of the red-shirted Apache trackers dismounted and pointed at the fresh tracks made by the horses when Julio departed and Desea rode back.

None of us opened up. We stayed hidden. The gang had guns drawn, and their horses spun in circles while the riders looked for somebody to shoot. Then the gang rode back between the canyon walls—out of our view. All was quiet again.

After ten minutes we saw tops of sombreros moving in the arroyo beside the road. We watched as six men climbed out of the arroyo and began moving up toward us, from rock to rock, heading toward where Boca and Desea lay in ambush.

We thought, Dios mio, the bandits are going to be on top of them if they do not shoot.

Then a flurry of pistol shots and then a rifle. One bandit ran, and one limped back to the arroyo. The others all had fallen, and we saw Boca, with a pistol in each hand, and Desea moving up the hill.

Louis, who had been counting, said that he thought the gang had already lost a third of its size. The three of us agreed that the bandits had surely had enough, but then we watched the entire bunch rush over the arroyo's edge and run to occupy the place Boca and Desea had just abandoned.

We readied our rifles, aiming at the spot where the bandits had gone into the rocks. Suddenly two emerged on the uphill side and began running. We fired and dropped one, and the other dived for cover. Then a volley came from the rest of the gang who were still in the place they had first run to. Teresa, Erasmo, and Domingo, around the corner of the rise, could see nothing of the fighting.

After ten or fifteens minutes of keeping us pinned down, Boca and Desea had climbed to a higher position on the other side of the bandits from us. We heard a rifle fire twice. Then, we saw the bandits moving around toward us again. We opened up. The attacking bandits were in a crossfire. They broke and ran back down and jumped into the arroyo beside the road.

Louis had climbed onto the top of the highest point by us. He said that he could see the heads of some of their horses. He suggested shooting at them, and we agreed it would further discourage the bandits from pressing their attack. We figured they had already had thirteen or so casualties, and to begin losing horses might make them leave. Desea was the only one to object to the shooting of the horses, but she could suggest no better plan.

The Englishman was a good shot. At the limits of the range of his rifle, but firing downhill, he brought down or wounded four horses before the bandits led their mounts to a deeper part of the arroyo, further from the mouth of the canyon.

For the remainder of the afternoon, the gang fired every so often in our direction. As the sun drifted low above the mountains, Boca and Desea appeared behind us. “They want something,” Boca said, “but none of us has anything valuable. Maybe it is revenge. I saw the leader. He is called El Casco—the father of El Viboro. He must know that you brothers are with us, and he wants you dead. What other reason could he be willing to chase us and lose so many men?"

We brothers said, "What if we leave tonight, and in the morning you tell him that we have gone. We could be across the river by noon tomorrow."

Boca placed his hand on his chin, but before he spoke we heard gunfire from the place where Teresa and the cousins were positioned. We heard shots from below, and we heard their shots. It was furious for a minute or two, then all the gunfire sounded from the arroyo the bandits occupied.

"That was a surprise for El Casco," declared Boca, "He now knows we are a dangerous bunch and not so easy to defeat."

We listened for more guns, but all was quiet again, then we heard Teresa who had worked her way toward us. She said, just loud enough for us to hear, "We downed three of them. Should we stay in our position or move up the hill?"

Louis and Boca looked at each other. Louis asked, "Do the local bandits attack at night? If so, we had best know where all of us are when it is dark, or we could shoot each other."

Boca answered Teresa, "Go back to your position and wait till almost dark, then all of you go to where Anna and Consuelo await."

As Teresa went back, Desea drew our attention to a white flag waving above the top of the bandit's arroyo. We watched as a man climbed onto the edge. Boca waved at him and the man began climbing toward us while he waved the flag so rapidly that the yucca stalk flying it broke in the middle and the flag fell onto the ground. The man retrieved the flag and continued to wave it in his hand.

About a hundred feet from us he stopped and said, "El Casco wants only one thing. El Casco wants the girl who was in the adobe when El Viboro was slain. He does not want to hurt her. Give him the girl and he will ride away and leave you in peace."

Us brothers said that El Casco must have heard of Consuelo's mission for the Holy Virgin. At the time, none knew why El Casco wanted Consuelo. Did he even know her name? Was he a religious man? We asked the flag waving man why was it that El Casco wanted the girl.

The man quit waving the flag and slowly wagged it with a puzzled look on his face. He wiped his brow with the flag and answered, "I do not know. But, he speaks very good things about her."

The flag man then looked oddly at Louis who asked him, in his Castilian accent, "Go and ask your boss why he wants the girl. Can you do that?"

He answered yes, then quickly made his way back to the arroyo. When he returned he said, "El Casco wants her to be a part of his family—like a daughter. Will you give her to him?"

Boca answered, "It is late. Let us talk in the morning. Tell your boss this must wait till then."

The bandit departed and we all retreated to the camp under the overhang. Desea built a fire while we told everyone the complete story—the ball of fire, Consuelo's obsession, and our pledge to assist her, so all there would know how fate had brought us to this situation.

Domingo stood the first guard, and the rest of us discussed what it was we should do. Boca said that he had known El Casco before the revolution, and that he owned land in Mexico. Boca said that El Casco was on the side of whomever's forces were closest–Carranza's or Villa's. But, he was a more compassionate man than his son El Viboro.

Consuelo wanted to go to the bandits. She pleaded, "That I go with them was meant to be. I carry a message, but it is not to be from my lips that the bandits will hear it."

None of us knew what she meant; not even us brothers, whose memory of the events in the well seemed to be something that never happened—except in our mind.

After midnight a veil of cloud moving from the west hid all but the brightest stars, then, when it was from horizon to horizon, it thickened like a blanket.

Morning came with only a gray-white, ambient light growing to become a gloomy, shadowless morning of heavy, damp stillness.

None of us saw Consuelo Alvarez leave, but all knew the gang of El Casco was no longer below us. Boca distributed the last strips of what he apologetically assured us was beef jerky.

CHAPTER 19

Some things are those you can experience and never hold, but Consuelo was a light and could be held; a light with a sweet warm breath. There are dreams which vanish by day, but she did not. Then, slowly, through days which each seemed a year, she was not in our thoughts all the time, and we again began to eat and work without her company. Finally, our guilt and regret only came into us when lying down to sleep, or when restless in the early hours before dawn.

Those with us that morning she had departed said we had no chance to bring her back. They were tired and glad to be alive. Jose wanted to return to his wife, and Teresa and Anna would accompany him to Boquillas. Boca said that El Casco's rancho was more than a hundred miles into Mexico, and that there were too many bandits and dangerous bands of soldiers riding for Carranza or Pancho Villa. Louis London agreed that we should all make it for the border as quickly as possible.

Boca and Desea said goodbye, and began walking to Boquillas. Erasmo and Domingo followed them, both riding the one horse they still had. After Boquillas, Louis planned to obtain another horse, then ride to Ojinaga and seek adventure with Villa's forces. Us brothers stood beside the road and said adios to all.

We felt the urge of our pledge to help Consuelo, so we followed the trail of El Casco. Each day the trail was older and she was farther away. It led to the southeast, toward Monclova, then, finally at a crest we looked out on the road winding into an empty hazy distance. We were starving and thirsty. We abandoned the search and turned around. We had talked ourselves into believing that God would continue to help her. After all, every danger she had faced while in our company was overcome with no help from us. We decided we had done all the Virgin expected of us, and that Consuelo had come and gone from our lives. She had enchanted us, and we would be slow to become lighthearted again. At that time we thought, never. Five days later we crossed the Rio Grande at Castolon.

We had little energy and were becoming hermits and living in an open jacal with a roof of reeds and ocotillo. Slowly through the winter we built adobe walls and made a better roof. We lived west of Castolon, close to Alamo Creek and the river. We did ranch work. The Texas Rangers knew us, as did the U. S. Army which patrolled the border.

In late March we planted a garden, but, before the end of that month, my brother moved away to the Mexican side and began to live in the abandoned casa of the Alvarez family. There was a sad kind of happiness to be where Consuelo had lived. One morning he went out our door. He took nothing with him but the clothes he wore. I was left with the adobe, the garden, our burro, and the memories we both carried.

It was in April that I heard my brother was ill. A short time later he died. I buried him close to the Alvarez graves. I made a coffin of boards and dug a grave in sand, and I built a dome of rocks above the grave.

Then, it was in late May of 1916 that I received the most miraculous news. It was after bandits had attacked in Glenn Springs during Cinco de Mayo. I was there with my cousin. That day he was first to notice a number of rough, mean looking men who the village had never seen before. We were not worried, even though many cattle had been stolen and herded into Mexico, and bandits had been seen on both sides of the river. U. S. soldiers lived at Glenn Springs, and Rangers were in and out all the time on their patrols.

The celebration was the usual dancing and music and drinking until the first shooting began. Before it was over, the small fort the soldiers had built was burned, and many of the dozen or so soldiers had been killed or wounded.

The bandits yelled "Viva Carranza" and "Viva Villa," like they were soldiers or rebels, but I think they were just renegades. My cousin had a shotgun, and for the entire raid his wife and children and him and me huddled behind an overturned table while he pointed the shotgun at the doorway. Nobody came, and after midnight the shooting stopped.

In the morning we saw the bandits, about two dozen, ride out with many horses loaded with loot from the store and the fort.

But, the miraculous news. It was that Consuelo Alvarez was found walking along a road, heading north, by a group of American soldiers and Texas Rangers who were into Mexico chasing bandits. She had told them that she was born in Boquillas on the Texas side, and she had been kidnaped by bandits who would not listen to her message from the Holy Virgin. One of the men with the Americans had known her father and said he remembered Consuelo, so they brought her with them to Boquillas del Carmen. From there she walked to the Rio Grande and crossed at Boquillas.

I traveled to Boquillas with my burro, Lucky, carrying trail supplies. Let me tell you now that it is bad luck for an animal to call it Lucky. That burro had already been named by the man who sold him to me. Lucky had no morning expectations of my words, and I have thought back many times that I should have turned that burro out into the desert to be wild with his kind.

Anyway, I arrived at the Boquillas store to find that Consuelo had departed for her family home. So, Lucky and I went there and found Consuelo. That evening she told me what had happened to her since last seeing us. Sitting by candles, after eating supper, she began her story:

She said that she had walked down to the bandits, and El Casco, whose name was Joaquin Vega, was very kind to her. They listened to the story of the light and heard her tell the reason she had come to them. Then she was put on a horse and taken many miles south. They were traveling to Joaquin Vega's rancho, but when they arrived after six days, it was found to be occupied by soldiers loyal to the Mexican government. They then rode into the mountains where they stayed through the winter.

After her first week with them, she became sick every morning, and Joaquin Vega became very much kinder to her, and he expected her to do no work. She was given a comfortable room. She had blankets and all the food she could eat. Finally, Consuelo discovered a secret from an old woman who helped her do everything. The woman said Consuelo was pregnant with the child of the eldest son of Joaquin Vega—Gilberto Ramon Apolinar Vega; who you know as El Viboro.

The woman's story told Consuelo something she had felt since departing Rancho de la Pared. Since that time she knew that somehow, but not by her, the message from the Virgin would purify the hearts of the bandits who had killed her family. As the woman spoke, Consuelo thought that the child within her was holy, because she thought herself a virgin. She had no memory of the son of Joaquin Vega.

The old woman who had befriended her departed. The oldest man in the camp began to cook the food, and Consuelo helped him. Some days Joaquin Vega and most of his men were gone. Consuelo liked doing the cooking. She said that she had needed something to do because they had expected no work from her, and the days of idleness were long.

The winter passed and she told me that the gift from God grew inside her and swelled her stomach.

On Cinco de Mayo everyone was in the mountain camp celebrating when three men rode in that afternoon. Joaquin Vega welcomed them. The cook, who was very drunk, told her as they both watched from a window that the men were the last of those who had ridden with El Viboro during his final days before death. He said that El Viboro was on a killing spree just before he met his end. He added, in a hushed voice, that nobody should say the name, El Viboro, to Joaquin Vega; he does not like that name for his son.

Consuelo thought these men were surely with El Viboro when her family was killed. She knew the Virgin expected her to help them to salvation. Then, Joaquin Vega entered and told the cook to find something for the arrivals to eat. The drunken cook staggered forward and caught himself from falling. Seeing that, Joaquin Vega looked at Consuelo and asked if she could prepare something for the new guests. She said yes, and both men went outside.

Consuelo discovered that almost everything had been eaten during supper. The goat bones had been thrown to the dogs and the platter of chicken was a pile of picked bones. So, she searched in the pantry, and in the back, behind a bag of corn, she discovered two tins with pictures of meat on the labels. Sweet Consuelo thought the travelers must be very hungry, so she chose the biggest can. It was a fat can with bulging sides and top. When she hammered a knife into the lid, the juices spewed out and bubbled. She heated tortillas and chili sauce while she cut away the lid. Then she made three plates of meat covered in chili sauce and rolled in tortillas.

The three grabbed the plates when she served them by their campfire. They wolfed the food, and one grunted and asked for more. All the short while they ate, Consuelo told them that she had been sent by the Holy Virgin to tell them they can still save their souls. She said her voice was not loud enough to be heard above their loud eating and conversation.

She went closer to them and was pushed away by one who looked coldly at her. He asked her if she was not the girl who fell into the well with Carlos? He said that he had been thinking that she was dead. He told her, "Come and give me a kiss, chica."

The man reached for her and she moved away. Then, Joaquin Vega came onto the scene. He placed himself between Consuelo and the man, and he told the man that he had welcomed him because he rode with his son. He told the man that he had eaten his food and that now the man had offended the mother of his grandson. Joaquin Vega then told the men to spend the night elsewhere. “Anywhere but in my camp,” he told them.

It was close to sundown. The three rode down the trail for a short ways and dismounted. One shouted back at Joaquin Vega and Consuelo. He said that they were are out of his camp. Then the man said, “Buenos noches.”

Consuelo waited an opportunity to go to them and again tell them the Virgin's message, but it was dark before she could leave without being missed. It was a short walk to their camp, and as she traveled she heard the Virgin's voice urging her on.

When she arrived, two seemed to be sleeping on the ground with no blankets or bedding. The third man, one who had not spoken with her, gurgled some sounds. He seemed unable to move. She threw a handful of grass onto the embers of their campfire, and in its light she saw a dying man and two dead men. Consuelo went to the dying man. His eyes were almost shut, and he lay with one arm under him and the other drawn up on his chest. She delivered the Virgin's message, but she did not think he heard it.

The next morning Joaquin Vega and his gang rode out. They took the three dead men away, carrying them across the horses the men rode in on. The cook told her that the canned meat was very old, that he was saving it for a special occasion, and that a swollen can is a bad sign.

The cook and Consuelo waited for over a week. Nobody returned. The cook said that it was probably that Joaquin Vega and his men had run into trouble, and that they were probably killed by government troops. The two then walked down through the mountains to the road. The cook went south and Consuelo began walking north to visit the graves of her family.

During the last nights in the mountains, she began having a recurring dream of being married by the Virgin. She remembered a man there with her in front of an altar of light. Then, in the last of the dream, on the night she last dreamed it, she said that she saw my face and heard my name.

Then she told me, "The child I carry is yours."

I stared at Consuelo with disbelief. Was I Juan or Pablo? I had no idea. I almost felt as though I was both. I said nothing to Consuelo who had moved her head against my chest and hugged me. Then, for a brief second a thought flew into my mind. It was the idea that I had chosen life over my death, then it was gone, along with a guilt that flew with it—a guilt which the thief feels. I knew I chose to be the brother who lived, and that my name was Juan Pablo. I lifted her head and held her face between my hands, and, looking into each other's eyes, I declared to Consuelo, I am Juan Pablo Luna.

She stared at me with tenderness and told me for the last time I ever heard the words from her lips, "I know who you are. You were sent by the Virgin."

That was all she said. Her words were not said without emotion. Did she know who I was? Was I not me? I never asked her to tell me, and from then on she called me Juan

Pablo.

We lived together in Castolon. We were safer there because bandits roamed freely in Mexico. We had neighbors, and the garden kept us fed. When asked by some local women, Consuelo told them that we had been married by the Holy Virgin, herself. Soon all believed us both to be a little loco but harmless.

We kept to ourselves. In July a son was born—Mario Louis Luna. I returned to our adobe from two days of work and found Consuelo with her baby.

We spent two more years there. Then one day in June of 1918, Consuelo decided to go visit the graves of her family. I was away working, so she left Mario Louis in the care of a family in Castolon. To this day I do not know why she did such a thing alone, with bandits and renegades on the Mexican side.

She did not return, and the next day I arrived home to hear the story told by a neighbor woman holding Mario Louis. She said Consuelo was supposed to return for the baby that morning, but she had not.

A vaquero who had been a soldier

accompanied me and we went to find her. He carried a rifle and handed a pistol to me.

That afternoon we found her body laying on the trail from the Alvarez adobe. There were no marks on her. She had not been shot or stabbed, and there was no new bumps on her head. There were some flowers in her hand. She appeared to have just laid down to sleep. Her eyes were closed and she had a look of contentment.

I stayed with her until the vaquero brought some more help. A woman worked over her for awhile, then said it appeared to be a natural death. She said that, maybe, it was her heart.

I built a coffin, and the next day she was buried by the grave of Juan Pablo. I extended his dome of rocks over her grave.

I grieved bitterly and hit the bottle. Mario Louis was given to live with my cousin from Glenn Springs. He and his family had moved to Alpine. They had lost two children to sickness in Glenn Springs. They accepted Mario Louis and raised him with their two remaining children.

Me, I moved to Terlingua and drank and

mined cinnabar for five years. Time passed and the bandits vanished along with the thin cover of growing things which once covered the rock. I looked out on a vista one day as I traveled the river road on my way to visit their graves. I had hiked up the Mariscal Mountain to cross it instead of following the road around. Up there I saw what the country had always been beneath a skin of dirt and grass. Its foundation was the rock. I had spent my life upon it. In the lowland deserts I had seen its mountains floating in the distance; raised up above shimmering silver air. I had slept upon it when sometime during each night the floating mountains would again settle upon their foundation rock so gently that their millions of tons came down unfelt. I looked around for its people and heard my father's words about the living being stored in the plants as spirits. At that moment I realized all who had died here were still here. Plants still grew here. Tough plants like the people had been. Beautiful plants full of spirits.

I became a different person after that. I quit drinking and came to visit Mario Louis in Alpine. Sometimes I traveled there every month. Before long he was married and had a child. She was called, Consuelo Maria Alvarez Luna. She was born in 1936. My cousin and me were happy grandfathers.

I met Margaret in Study Butte. She was the first to suggest that I harvest cactus of a pretty kind. It was lucky for me that I met her, because of the many things my search for cactuses led me to discover. Even this place. When I completed this casa, I dug the graves here and moved Consuelo and Juan Pablo. My burro, Conmigo, carried each coffin. That burro was a decent listener, and his attention to my words kept my talking-self and my listening-self from becoming two people.

Cactus Man's last words of his story were, "So that is my story for now. I am tired and must sleep."

CHAPTER 20

I found myself awake with my head on the table and my pencil still in my hand. I straightened up and yawned and stretched. It was morning and I had awakened to see the yellow morning air the same brightness as the kerosene light gave to the interior. It was like the lights on the table were also lighting the area outside the dome; all the way to the elephants.

I looked to see Cactus Man in his bed, but he was not in it. I had a feeling of apprehension as I went to the entry door, called out, and heard no reply. I went to the doorway leading to the reservoir below. I called his name. No reply.

I felt anxious when I went outside the dome. Then, I saw his grave to be. Oh, God. It was filled. The dammed dirt had poured in, and I was sure the cactus Man was under it, because Vagabundo stood facing the filled grave. His head was lowered and he was unmoving.

I dropped onto my knees and began to frantically dig at the earth covering the grave. But a jumble of loose boards made digging impossible.

Tears came as I thought, “So, it is ended.”

I recalled some words the Cactus Man had said during the night, “The Big Bend, a land of sun and stone, where people are few, and you may have to die alone.” I felt that the Big Bend was hollow with the loss of his knowledge of its every secret, and I imagined forlorned spirits gathered invisibly around the grave of the man who had so often brought them to life. The morning breeze was their breath, and it passed through me as if I were gauze. I thought and heard the words in my skull, “O Earth, what changes thou hast seen.”

The sun had found me before I returned inside. I sat down and read some of the story, then I wrote a while and made coffee. Then I carefully replaced the beans of his diary into their respective bags and tins, and set them back into the drawers and shelves of the hutch. In one drawer I found a round tin container like something that would have held a fruitcake. It was light, as though empty, but out of curiosity I opened it. Inside it I discovered a rolled, white cloth bandage. I held it up and let it unroll toward the floor. I stood there, staring at a series of old, now browned, spots of blood, and I recalled the Cactus Man's description of the bandage torn from Consuelo's foot in the escape from El Viboro's camp.

Until finding the bandage I had wondered, sometimes skeptically, about the veracity of Cactus Man's tales, but in that moment I understood that all he told was truth. Fate truly did not know the next card to be dealt, and could not plan a person's life even in the isolation of the Big Bend, where lives lived on the edge of the world would seem to be so predictable. I rolled the bandage and replaced it in the tin; thinking that if time magically returned the world to 1900, and began another journey to the present, there would probably be no bandage, or me to know it ever could have existed. Cactus Man was right—Fate did not know his own fate. No lifetime, no day, no hour could be duplicated.

I gathered up my things and placed

them into the pack. I thought that the first thing to do was to drive to Alpine and search for Cactus Man's son, Mario Luna, or Mario's daughter, Consuelo Maria—she would be my age. Cactus Man's cousin who had raised Mario in Alpine might still be alive, I thought. Maybe I could call and see if he was listed. I also planned on calling Margaret in El Paso.

I shut both halves of the entry door and walked to the head of the cactus-roofed trail. I stepped into the corridor, then I remembered the mesquite seedling which was supposed to end up on top of the graves. I had not noticed it. Was it under the dirt?

I returned to the graves and began to dig through the soil. I felt the little tree and carefully removed the dirt above it and lifted it up so its leaves could be in the air.

When I was finished, the tree looked like it had grown there. Then, I went down the winding steps to the reservoir and brought back a full bucket of water.

I poured the water around the mesquite tree's slender stem. Remaining on my knees I said out loud, Little fellow if you only knew what was in store for you as a spirit vessel.

The times you will have.

A woman's voice from behind said, “Yes. If it only knew. You must be Gene Hart. Margaret remembered me and telephoned.”

I turned and looked up, but the sun was above the figure, and all I could see was a silhouette beneath its light. Then I stood and saw Consuelo Maria Alvarez—the image of her grandmother.

Fate had turned another card.

The End

www.ingramcontent.com/pod-product-compliance
Lightning Source LLC
LaVergne TN
LVHW050617100826
845148LV00011B/1630

* 9 7 8 0 9 7 9 9 7 2 3 2 4 *